ST.

THE ~~LAND OF GEMS~~ IS

A Trilogy

Book One
The Ride of Doom

Anthony Pardoe
in collaboration with
Suzanne Pardoe

ISBN-13: 978-1517025922
ISBN-10: 1517025923

If the adventures of Star and Jasper delight and excite,
and carry you along on a wave of suspense,
this book is dedicated to you.

For if this happens, you are blessed
with a wonderful imagination!

With this imagination,
you can build a castle of dreams,
and go anywhere you please.

Spin rainbows for the common good, and your
life will sparkle!

Anthony Pardoe

CONTENTS

For an illustrated colour glossary of the gemstones and crystals mentioned in the trilogy, and other exciting information, visit Star and Jasper's website

StarJasper.com

Chapter One

A Life-Changing Decision

'I hate you! I wish you'd disappeared instead of Dad!'

Star immediately regretted her words, as her mum rushed into the house in tears.

The argument – which had started during breakfast, simmered through the morning and exploded again at lunch – had now reached its usual conclusion, and despair replaced Star's anger – a despair that was happening more and more often since her dad went missing.

Why is life so unfair? she thought miserably. *Why should I have a mum who hates me, and why should my dad just disappear?*

Before her calm, reliable, fun-loving dad left on his last prospecting trip to South America, her life had been happy and carefree, but when the news came that he was missing – that he'd gone into the jungle and not come out – all the fun and joy in her life had disappeared with him. She'd lost all her confidence, and was beginning to withdraw into a shell, just like her mum, though she knew her core ideals – like keeping her word and following things through to the end – were as strong as ever.

Star had been a friendly, inquisitive girl who loved school and shared her dad's interest in crystals and minerals, but a long winter had now descended upon her world and not even the warm late summer sun could change that – which is why she really needed to go swimming. It was a way of keeping in touch with her dad, and she needed that today.

What IS the point, she thought, *of having a house by the sea, with its own private path to the beach, if you can't go swimming when the sun shines?*

Star loved swimming more than anything else, and some of her happiest memories were when her dad would scoop her up out of the blue, and take her to the beach.

'Come on Star,' he'd say, 'let's go swimming!'

They would race each other to the bottom of the garden, rush through the wicker gate, along the short path through the trees, run across the shingle beach that stretched away to become part of the Jurassic Coast, and dive into the cool, clear water!

For a moment the memory made her smile, but as she remembered she was forbidden to go swimming until her summer homework was finished, her anger returned. She and her mum were very different, but even so, she wondered why they argued so much because it hadn't always been this way.

Star knew she was like her dad – intelligent, warm, and loving. Okay – her mum was kind and loving, and warm and intelligent too, but since the tragedy she'd retreated into a shell and become overprotective and bossy. Star felt stifled, and with her dad gone, had no outlet for her personality. She longed to be herself again.

Take today's argument, for instance. It had begun when, in response to her mum saying it was going to be a nice day, Star had mentioned that she wanted to take a picnic to the beach – and this had resulted in the usual bucket of cold water thrown over her plans.

'You can't go swimming today, Star,' her mum had replied firmly. 'You said you'd start your project today, and I'm holding you to that.'

Star glared at her mother. She HAD said she'd start her project today, but yesterday the forecast was for rain. How was she to know that the forecast would be wrong? And how was she to know that she'd wake up, see the sunshine streaming through the curtains and feel a real need to do the one thing that still gave her pleasure – go swimming, like she used to do with her dad?

'Mum, I NEED to go to the beach today,' she'd pleaded, 'it's important to me.'

'Well you can't,' her mum had replied shortly, 'and that's that.'

Star had felt cheated. She really longed to sit on the beach, dream of her dad, and the adventures that had made her life so exciting.

How can she be so unreasonable? she'd asked herself miserably. *She just doesn't get it.*

For a while Star sat at the wooden table, still covered with the remains of lunch, listening to the waves lapping the pebble beach and the soft sounds of summer filtering through the canopy of leaves into the secluded garden. It was the kind of day where the bees buzz softly and the birds sing quietly, and eventually the warm sun took the edge off her anger and she began to doze.

Her mother returned and smiled at Star as she cleared the table, making a big effort to defuse the situation.

'I'll bring your books and you can do your project here in the garden,' she said.

'Don't want to,' muttered Star as her mum took the dishes away, though she knew she had no choice. Her mum was going to make her do her homework, come what may.

It wasn't that she didn't WANT to do her homework – just not today. She'd chosen the project herself on one of her favourite subjects – gemstones and crystals – and she knew she'd have to start it soon because the school holidays were nearly over, but NOT today. Today she wanted to go swimming, and then sit on the beach and think of her dad.

Her interest in crystals ran in the family. Apart from her dad, she had an uncle who was a prospector in far-off Australia and another who was the curator of a mineral museum, filled with breathtakingly beautiful crystals, and she'd loved the way they would tell tales of finding caves filled with crystals and opals on their prospecting trips. She had even been named after a gemstone – her name was "Star Sapphire", though she preferred to be called "Star".

Her mum returned with her project books, and laid them on the garden table.

'Here's the book your uncle sent. It's one of the most beautiful books I've ever seen, with photos of all the gemstones and lots of other information. It's bound to help.'

Star, still angry at being denied swimming, replied sullenly, 'I can't concentrate in this heat. I need to go to the beach, so I'm GOING.'

'NO WAY!' came the angry retort. 'You're staying here until you've finished your project, and that will take the rest of today and all of tomorrow – and that's if you work hard.'

Petulantly, Star kicked at a small oval pebble at her feet, and pleaded, 'Pleeeeeeeease? Just for today?'

Her mum was firm.

'NO! You are going to do your project, and until you've finished you're staying here. No swimming and no going to the beach until your homework is done. If you don't start your homework today you'll get no supper and you'll be grounded until it's finished. THAT'S FINAL.'

Her mother stalked off, leaving Star glaring miserably at her project books, thinking how unfair the world was, and whether one match would be enough to light a house, but soon the gentle sounds of summer and the faint lapping of the waves on the shingle beach beyond the garden made her feel sleepy. She closed her eyes and began to doze.

She woke to find her mother's arms around her shoulders, giving her a gentle hug.

'Come on Star, let's not argue. You know you have to do it and you can go swimming this weekend. Let's be friends?' she said, doing her best to smile.

Star shrugged her off, still in her petulant mood.

'Don't sulk, Star. It's too nice a day to sulk,' said her mother, opening the book of gemstones and placing it in front of Star. 'I'll leave you to it, but call me if I can help.'

She walked into the house, leaving Star glaring at the pictures in her book.

Morosely, she kicked again at the small pebble near her feet, and then her phone rang.

'Oh Hi, Julia. No, I can't go out today. Stupid homework. She says if I don't do it I'll be grounded. She makes me SO angry! Okay, see you Saturday. Bye.'

Reluctantly, she pulled the book towards her and began to read. Each page had a spectacularly beautiful photo of a gem, crystal or mineral, with its name printed in large letters and a diagram of its crystal form. Beginning her revision, she read the names of the stones aloud so as to remember them: '**Amethyst, Aquamarine, Azurite, Black Onyx, Bloodstone, Blue Lace Agate, Botswana Agate, Chrysophrase, Citrine, Crazy Lace Agate, Diamond, Emerald, Garnet, Jasper, Lapis Lazuli, Moss Agate, Opal, Peridot, Rock Crystal, Rose Quartz, Ruby, Sapphire, Tiger's Eye, Topaz.**'

Finishing the section on crystals, she began to read the names of the mineral ores: '**Iron Pyrite,** also known as Fool's Gold, **Galena**, an ore of lead and silver, **Cassiterite**, an ore of tin, **Chalcopyrite**, an ore of copper, **Pitchblende**, an ore of uranium, black, crumbly and radioactive.'

She finished the book, took a deep breath and began again, but as she read aloud, the names of the stones seemed to meld in with the sound of the waves and the gentle murmur of the summer garden. Her voice became quieter, and the sound of the bees and distant waves grew softer and softer until her eyes closed and her head nodded forward.

She opened her eyes with a start, and continued, '**Amethyst, Aquamarine, Azurite**... **Azurite**... **Azurite**...' but then the senses and sounds of summer overwhelmed her and she closed her eyes, leaned forward with her head on her arms, and fell fast asleep.

*

She heard a small but clear voice.

'Help!'

She opened her eyes, saw nothing but the familiar garden and then, lulled by the sound of the bees and the waves breaking gently on the shingle beach, drifted back to sleep.

'Help!'

The voice came again, more insistently. She opened her eyes, and as it seemed to be coming from somewhere near her feet, glanced down. She saw nothing, and in the warmth of the familiar garden, drifted back to sleep.

The voice came again, louder this time.

'Help!'

Star opened her eyes and this time saw a small, smooth oval pebble gazing up at her imploringly. She stared at it for a while, then thought, *I'm dreaming*, and closed her eyes.

The voice came again, loud and pleading.

'Help! Please help!'

This time she gazed down at the pebble with interest and surprise.

It had small arms, tiny ears and hands, honest-looking eyes set in an endearingly expressive face, and was gazing up at her with the most beautiful smile she had ever seen, displaying two rows of perfect little white teeth.

'I'm not dreaming,' she said to herself. And then, to the pebble, 'Yes?'

The pebble looked relieved and said, 'I need your help. Please?'

Star gazed at the pebble, with its white teeth sparkling in the sun and said, matter-of-factly, 'You're a pebble.'

'Yes,' replied the pebble, still looking up at Star imploringly. 'Pleeeeease?'

'But you're a pebble,' she responded, in a slightly exasperated tone of voice.

'Yes I am, but I need your help. I really need your help,' it replied hopefully.

'HOW?' asked Star, still not moving from her comfortable sleepy position, with her head on her arms, leaning on the wooden table.

8

'By taking me back to my friends on the beach,' replied the pebble, adding sadly, 'I miss my friends. It's so lonely here without them. Friends are so important to me.'

'Me too,' replied Star. 'I'd miss my friends if they went away – but why are you here in my garden and all your friends on the beach?'

*

The pebble went on, as if repeating a speech learnt by heart, 'I live on the beach with the other pebbles, my friends...'

'No you don't,' cut in Star, 'you live here, in my garden.'

The pebble looked crestfallen, but went on, 'Er... well yes, I do NOW, but only because the sea went out when I was asleep, and when I woke up it had gone, taking all my friends with it. It's a long story, but...'

Star cut the pebble short. 'It's too hot for long stories,' she said, closing her eyes.

She was just drifting off to sleep when she heard the sound of sobbing, and when she opened her eyes, saw that the pebble was looking utterly miserable, rubbing its eyes with the back of its hands, its tears evaporating in the warm afternoon sun. With a feeling of regret she sat up and bent down towards the pebble.

'I'm sorry, little pebble. I didn't mean to upset you. I AM interested in your story, really I am. I... I WOULD like to hear your story, however long.'

The pebble brightened, blew its nose on a very small handkerchief and smiled. 'Well, a long time ago…'

Star interrupted with, 'How long?' at which the pebble became flustered again.

'Hmm, I don't know, but it was a long time. Maybe a thousand years, maybe ten. I'm not sure, because I was asleep for most of the time.'

Star tried – and failed – to suppress a giggle, and the pebble looked crestfallen.

'Please go on, Pebble,' she said. 'I AM interested.'

'Well, for many years (Star suppressed the urge to ask 'How many?') I lived with all my friends on a pebble beach. In those days the sea levels were higher you know, and the beach was here, where your garden is now. But one day I fell asleep, and when I woke up, the sea had gone! Yes, gone! And so had all my friends. I was completely alone, so I went to sleep again, expecting it to come back – I sleep a lot, you know – but it didn't and I have been here ever since. Until…' it said in a rather puzzled voice, 'until something woke me up just now.'

'Something woke you up, after all this time?' asked Star incredulously.

'Yes, it felt like a kick. It happened twice. The first time I thought I was dreaming, but the second time it woke me up,' replied the pebble.

Realising that she had kicked the pebble during the argument with her mum, Star couldn't help smiling, though she did her best to suppress it.

'So the sea level dropped while you were asleep,

and left you high and dry?'

'YES!' cried the pebble excitedly, 'that's EXACTLY what happened.'

'And when the sea went away, what was once the beach became my garden?' she asked.

'Yes, that's what happened. That's exactly what happened,' replied the pebble. 'I know my friends are near because I can hear them chattering when the waves come in, but I'm stuck here. I miss my friends so much,' it went on sadly.

'But Pebble, I don't understand. When you found the sea had gone, why didn't you just go back to the beach by yourself?'

'**I CAN'T**,' wailed the pebble. 'Pebbles can't walk.'

'But you've got arms, ears, a nice smile and lovely little teeth...' said Star.

'**BUT NO LEGS**,' finished the pebble, sadly.

'Why not?' asked Star in surprise. 'What happened to them?'

'Sea Pebbles don't have legs,' it replied.

'Why not?' she asked.

'I don't know,' it responded, 'perhaps they'd get rubbed off. We get washed from one ocean to another so we don't really need them.'

Star continued to gaze at the pebble, with its open honest face, its warm engaging smile and sparkling little teeth. The pebble returned Star's gaze, its little eyes looking up at her earnestly.

'**PLEASE** take me back to the beach, so I can be with my friends. Please?' it implored.

Star couldn't help smiling, though she knew she couldn't help the pebble, recalling the argument she'd had with her mum, which had left them both in tears. She had homework to do, and was forbidden from going to the beach until it was finished. She dared not disobey.

'Pebble, I've heard of people missing the bus,' she said, with a smile, 'but to miss the SEA – wow! That's pretty incredible.'

The pebble, looking embarrassed again, mumbled, 'I do sleep a lot,' adding, in an even quieter voice, 'I'm only a pebble.' Gazing at Star with its most imploring look, it wailed, 'Pleeeeeeease? Pleeeeeease?'

'Pebble, I can't,' she replied. 'I'm supposed to be doing my homework. I just had a huge argument with my mum and if she finds I've gone to the beach I'll be grounded and get no supper. I'd like to help, but I can't take you back to be with your friends. Not today, anyway.'

At the word "supper" the pebble produced a small winkle shell bag with a leather strap, and took out a tiny scrap of dried seaweed. Looking up at Star with the same imploring expression, it began to munch.

'Pleash?' it asked.

'Don't speak with your mouth full, Pebble,' replied Star with mock severity, mimicking the phrase so often used by her mum.

The pebble finished its seaweed, took out a very small handkerchief, and blew its nose.

'Please?' it asked imploringly. 'I'm so lonely. I miss my friends so much.'

Star gazed at the pebble for a while, and the more she did the more she realised that she wanted to help, especially as she knew that she had been the one to wake it from its long sleep. She knew how much she would miss HER friends if they all went away and she knew how much she missed her dad – who'd been her best friend.

'Why are you smiling and crying at the same time?' asked the pebble anxiously, bringing her back from her thoughts.

'I was thinking of my dad, Pebble. He was my best friend and he used to love his friends, and being on the beach too, so I know how you feel. I've wanted to go to the beach all day, and I'd really like to take you back, but my mum won't let me and if she finds out I've gone, my life won't be worth living.'

'Oh dear,' replied the pebble sadly, 'I don't want you to be in trouble because of me. I'll just stay here, and hope the sea comes back one day.'

'The sea won't come back, Pebble!' Star replied with a smile, but it had lapsed into silence, and she could see it was rubbing its eyes, trying to hold back the tears.

Gazing at the pebble, she felt a surge of tenderness which she couldn't quite explain.

'If I take you back…' she began – and immediately the pebble brightened and looked up, its eyes full of hope.

'IF I take you back…' she began again.

It was no use pretending. The innocent little pebble, who wanted so much to be with its friends, but didn't want to get Star into trouble, had won her over!

'Okay, Pebble,' she said, 'I'll take you to the beach, but we'll have to be QUICK! Very, very quick, before Mum finds out I've gone. We'll have to run.'

The pebble gave a whoop of joy, gathered its belongings into the little winkle shell bag, strapped it on like a satchel and held out its hand. Star, who was wearing her favourite clothes – a blue artist's smock with a front pocket and blue jeans – lifted it up with both hands, and smiled. The pebble gave her a wonderful, warm smile in return.

'Thank you!' it said happily. 'I can't WAIT to see my friends again.'

'Pebble,' said Star, 'I'm going to put you in my pocket so you don't fall out.'

As Star slipped the pebble into her smock pocket, she felt it grab the sides with both tiny hands, and peer out over the top so it could see where they were going. It looked for all the world like a baby kangaroo peering out of its mother's pouch, and Star couldn't help remarking, 'Pebble, you look just like a baby kangaroo!'

The pebble looked up happily, and with the most endearing little smile she had ever seen, asked, 'What's a baby kangaroo?'

'Never mind, Pebble,' replied Star, anxious to get going, 'but you look just like one!'

With a last look around to make sure her mum wasn't looking, Star turned quickly and half-walked, half-ran to the wicker gate at the bottom of the garden leading to the path through the trees, with the pebble peering out of her smock pocket, looking happy and excited. She could hear the waves lapping the shingle beach, and as she opened the gate the pebble gave a squeal of delight. Star smiled – a warm and satisfied smile, because she knew she was doing the right thing – and if her mum found out, well, that was just too bad.

Chapter Two

The Sand Makers

Star passed through the gate – and stopped in alarm!

What's happening? she thought, noticing that the trees, now blocking the sun and making the path dark and forbidding, were a lot higher than she remembered, and the path overgrown with weeds and bushes.

'How could this be?' she asked herself. 'It wasn't like this yesterday.'

The pebble looked up anxiously and asked, 'Is anything wrong?'

'I don't know,' she replied. 'It just doesn't look familiar, that's all, but we can still hear the sea, and I KNOW this path leads to the beach because I've used it hundreds of times.'

Star knew how much the pebble wanted to be with its friends, so although the waves seemed more distant and the path didn't look right, she began to push her way through the undergrowth, wondering why the path should be so gloomy on such a sunny day.

The pebble looked up excitedly.

'I can smell the sea! It can't be far!' it said happily, fending off with its little arms the fronds of undergrowth that were brushing against its face.

A slight tremor of fear crept into Star's voice.

'It's not far, Pebble,' she replied, and then, more to herself, 'it CAN'T be far.'

She pressed on, pushing through the undergrowth, looking anxiously at the gloomy forest of trees, an unexpected wind sighing through the branches – not like she remembered at all – wondering how such a short path could be so long and how the well-worn path she used yesterday could be so overgrown today. It just didn't make sense. She knew the path like the back of her hand, but… it wasn't familiar any more. For a moment she stopped and thought of turning back, but hearing the waves lapping the shingle and knowing how much the pebble wanted to get to the beach, she decided to press on.

The pebble, trusting and happy, peered out of her pocket, enjoying the experience!

The path seemed to go on for ages, but suddenly came to an abrupt end, the sun came out with all its warmth and her spirits rose.

'Not far now, Pebble,' she said brightly, relieved to be out of the gloom.

Everything seemed more like she remembered, except… except the path didn't end at the shingle beach as she expected. Instead, she was faced by an enormous sand dune, which completely blocked her way – very high and steep and covered with bushes and small trees. Star stopped in alarm. In front of the sand dune, going to the left and to the right, was a new path that she couldn't remember seeing before.

'That's funny, Pebble,' she mused, trying to keep the anxiety out of her voice, 'I've been here hundreds of times, but I don't remember this path and I certainly don't remember this sand dune. I'm sure it wasn't here last time. It's too steep to climb so we can't go over it. We'll just have to go around it.'

The pebble, with a cheerful, trusting look, replied, 'It can't be far. I can hear my friends chattering when the waves come in.'

'No, Pebble, it's not far,' Star replied with more confidence than she felt. 'The beach is just the other side of this sand dune, but we have to find a way to get around it before we can get there.'

She looked to the left, and then to the right, trying to make up her mind which of the two paths would be the quicker way to get past the sand dune and reach the sea.

'Pebble,' she said, 'we have to make a decision. Shall we take the left path or the right? Which way shall we go?'

'Why don't you ASK? That's what I'm here for,' came a weary voice from behind.

Startled, Star spun round and saw, for the first time, the most decrepit signpost she had ever seen. Her mouth open in surprise, she stared at it, noticing that it had two arms, one pointing to the left and the other to the right, both drooping so much that the ends were lost in the undergrowth.

It wore a resigned, confused look and she continued gazing at it until the signpost, rather abruptly, said, 'Don't stare. It's rude.'

Star gave an involuntary little start, and gathering her wits, replied, 'I'm sorry. I... I didn't mean to stare, but I've been here so many times – and I've never noticed a signpost here before.'

'Can't help that,' said the signpost brusquely. 'I've always been here. If you haven't noticed me, you're not very good at noticing, is all I can say.'

'Well,' she replied in a puzzled voice, 'I always knew the way to the beach, but... but now... it all seems so different. I'm trying to get Pebble to the beach so it can be with its friends, and get back before my mum finds I've gone. Can you tell me the quickest way?'

'Perhaps,' responded the signpost indifferently, lapsing into an uninterested silence.

Star thought this was rude and so, deciding to find out for herself, began to read its drooping arms. This wasn't easy, because the writing was old and faded, but eventually she managed to decipher the sign pointing to the left, and read "TO THE OLD ABANDONED MINE".

She shivered, as if struck by a cold wind, and said, 'I don't like the sound of that, Pebble. My dad used to explore old mines, but they always frightened me. An old abandoned mine! I wouldn't like to go there. Ugh!' Then, remembering something, she said, 'Wait a minute! I remember my uncle telling me that there was an old lead mine somewhere around here, but it was abandoned years ago and now nobody knows where it is. Perhaps this is it.'

She turned to look at the other sign, the one pointing to the right, and after a while managed to read "THE SEA – A LONG WAY". She looked at the signpost, which was still regarding her without much interest, and asked, 'Please... which way is the sea? I mean, which is the QUICKEST way to the sea?'

The signpost yawned. 'Uh?'

'The sea,' replied Star more firmly, 'which way is the SEA?'

For a while the signpost seemed to be lost in thought, but then lifted its arm slightly and pointed to the path on the left.

'That way,' it said firmly.

Star looked down the path, then back to the signpost.

'But that's the way to the abandoned mine,' she said anxiously.

'Can't help that,' replied the signpost abruptly, looking even less interested.

She glanced down at the pebble, who was regarding the signpost with a mixture of curiosity and amusement.

'I don't want to go to a spooky old mine, Pebble, but if that's the quickest way to the beach, that's the way we'll have to go.'

She turned to thank the signpost, but it was now completely uninterested and had looked away, so Star began to walk along the path, slowly picking her way through the small bushes, weeds and trees that made it almost impassable. She hadn't gone far, however, before she was stopped in her tracks by the signpost, calling out pathetically, 'Or... or it might be that way.'

Star turned and saw that the signpost was now pointing to the other path.

'Make up your mind,' she said, and in a very exasperated voice added, 'Don't you KNOW?'

'No,' it replied, looking embarrassed and sheepish.

'But you're a SIGNPOST,' she said, walking back. 'You are SUPPOSED to know. This is ridiculous.'

'Yes, I know. I agree,' it replied sadly.

Star looked at the pebble, who was staring at the signpost with the ghost of a smile, and said, 'Pebble, looks like WE'LL have to choose which way to go. The signpost can't help us.'

The pebble nodded, and asked, 'Are all signposts like this? Doesn't seem very useful to me.'

'They're not usually as bad as this,' she replied, and then turning to the signpost and pointing down the path to the abandoned mine, went on. 'According to you this is the way to the old abandoned mine...'

'Is it? Is that what it says?' interrupted the signpost, looking interested for the first time.

Taken aback, Star replied, 'Yes. Yes, that's what it says. Don't you KNOW?'

'No. I never learned to read,' said the signpost and then, sadly and pathetically, 'I wish I could read.'

'Well, now that you know what it says,' replied

Star, 'you don't need to be able to read. All you need to do is remember.'

'But my remembering is worse than my reading,' wailed the signpost inconsolably.

'Oh dear,' replied Star in exasperation, 'in that case there's no point in holding your arms out. You may as well put them down.'

'You think so? Can I?' asked the signpost, brightening and looking left and right, as if to make sure no-one was watching. 'Can I, really?'

'You may as well,' replied Star, at which the signpost slowly lowered its arms.

'Aaaaaah. What a relief! Oh, that feels so good! Aaaaaah. I wish I'd thought of that.'

The pebble looked at Star, and she could see it was trying hard not to laugh.

'Has it really had its arms up all this time for nothing?' it asked. 'I don't think it's very intelligent. We ought to say something.'

'I agree, Pebble, but there's no point upsetting it,' replied Star.

'The sea sounds louder this way,' she remarked, looking at the signpost and pointing to the path on the left, 'so we'll... er... say goodbye.'

'And ... er ... thanks for your help,' she added as an afterthought.

'That's alright,' said the signpost happily. 'Glad to have been of assistance. That's what I'm here for.'

'I can't BELIEVE it's held its arms up all this time for nothing,' said the pebble, rolling its little eyes.

'How ridiculous is that?

With one last look at the signpost, Star began to walk along the path towards the old abandoned mine, threading her way between the weeds, shrubs and small trees. The further she went, the more overgrown it became, and she came to the conclusion that the path hadn't been used for years. Eventually she stopped and glanced back at the signpost, wondering if the other way would have been better, but it was scratching itself and didn't see her, so she decided to press on.

'Come on, Pebble,' she said decisively. 'We can hear the sea. It can't be far now. Let's get on as fast as we can.'

*

Star continued to struggle through the undergrowth, listening to the sound of the waves lapping on the pebble beach beyond the towering sand dune, and before long came to a place where the path entered a narrow cutting between the high dune on her right, and a steep rock face which had appeared on her left. The path became colder and more mysterious and the undergrowth so thick that she could hardly push her way through. She found it very difficult to keep the brambles away from the pebble's face.

For a while she struggled on, hoping it would get easier and looking for any sign that the path might lead to the beach, but before long it ended in an impenetrable mass of brambles, and she had to stop. She had reached an impasse.

'Pebble, no-one has been here for ages,' Star said anxiously. 'We can't get through these brambles so we'll have to go back. Maybe the other path will be better, but this is not how it should be. Something is wrong, but I don't know what. We should have been on the beach ages ago.'

She looked up at the sand dune, which didn't seem quite as steep here, and wondered if she could climb it.

'I might be able to climb the sand dune, Pebble. It's not as steep here and it would certainly be quicker. Or we can go back and try the other path.'

The pebble, catching the anxiety in her voice, looked up sharply, but Star had already made her decision. With more confidence than she felt, she said, 'We can hear the waves and we know the sea is close, but we'll go back the way we came. It may be longer, but you'll soon be with your friends.'

Holding the pebble securely in her pocket, she turned and was about to make her way back when she felt a strange cool breeze on her face. It seemed to come from nowhere, and it was strong enough to ruffle her hair and waggle the pebble's little ears.

She stopped in surprise and said, more to herself than the pebble, 'Where IS this breeze coming from? It's weird – it seems to be coming from nowhere.'

Looking around, she saw the trees and bushes by the rock face moving restlessly, and although she couldn't see where the wind was coming from, she knew it had to be from somewhere behind the bushes, and that meant it must somehow be coming from out of the rocks. Wanting to move on, but fascinated by the strange wind and curious to know where it was coming from – she hesitated for a moment, and then parted the bushes to see what lay behind.

The sight that met her eyes caused her to cry out in surprise. Behind the bushes and ferns was an overgrown cutting, going deep into the hillside. Silent and mysterious, and strewn with moss-covered rocks and rusty old tools, what really surprised her was the sight, at the end of the cutting, of a dark and mysterious tunnel! Festooned with ferns that were rustling and moving gently in the cool breeze coming out of the entrance, it all looked very spooky.

'Pebble,' she said anxiously, 'this must be the old lead mine. It must have been abandoned years ago. No-one has been here for ages.'

She shivered, not so much from the cool breeze as from the feeling that she had stepped back in time, and although she was frightened, she couldn't help being fascinated by the old underground workings, long reclaimed by nature. Running out of the dark mine tunnel were the rails of an old mine tramway, and at the side of the cutting, sitting on more rusty rails, was an old mine truck – the sort miners used to use in the old days to push ore and rock out of a mine.

'Pebble,' she said quietly, 'men used to work here, but now it's abandoned and forgotten. Look how old and rusty everything is. Nothing has been touched for years.'

The pebble, looking at Star anxiously, said in a small voice, 'It frightens me. Can we go now?'

'Yes, me too, Pebble,' she replied, shivering again. 'Let's get back to the sunshine and find the beach.'

Star took one last look at the quiet, fascinating scene, abandoned by man and overtaken by nature, with its riot of ferns hanging over the dark entrance, moving gently in the breeze coming from somewhere deep within the old workings.

'I'd hate to go in there, Pebble. It's too scary for words. Let's get out of here,' she said, backing away.

She was about to make her way back to the signpost when she became aware that the sound of the waves lapping the shingle beach seemed much louder than before, and paused.

'Pebble, we can hear the waves and,' she went on in a puzzled voice, 'they seem much louder than before.'

'Yes, they do!' cried the pebble excitedly. 'And I can hear my friends! I can't wait!'

'Maybe I CAN climb it,' she said, looking again at the dune. 'There are trees and bushes I can hold on to. What do you think? Shall I have a go?'

'YES!' cried the pebble. 'I'm sure you can do it.'

'Come on then, Pebble! Hold tight! We'll have a go.'

*

Star began to climb the sand dune, threading her way through the bushes and small trees, holding the pebble securely in her pocket with one hand and pulling herself up with the other. It wasn't easy because of the soft sand, and not only did she find it very hard going, but the further she went the steeper it became, which puzzled her. Spurred on by the sound of the waves, she continued to climb, but the sand dragged at her feet, making her tired, and soon she was out of breath. She HAD to get back before her mum found she was missing, but saw with alarm that not only did the dune seem to be getting steeper, it also seemed to be getting higher, which didn't make sense.

Flopping down on the sand with her back to a tree, she tried to catch her breath.

'Pebble,' she panted, 'we must be nearly at the top, but what I don't understand is that it seems to be getting higher and steeper the further we go. I just can't make it out.'

At first, her panting drowned out even the sound of the waves, but as she calmed down and her breath came more easily, Star became aware of strange voices coming from further up the dune, and an odd whirring and grinding sound. She listened to the voices for a while, and wondered what could be making such an unusual noise.

The voices – there were two of them – were saying, 'There's one! Grab it!'

'Yep, got it!'

Then came the strange whirring, grinding noise that reminded Star of her mum's electric blender.

'I wonder who's talking and what that noise is, Pebble,' she said, looking down at her pocket, but not seeing the pebble.

'Pebble?' she asked anxiously.

The pebble had disappeared, and was deep inside her pocket, with only its little eyes showing from time to time as it peered up anxiously. It was shaking like a leaf, and in a weak and frightened voice said, 'Let's go back? Please? Please?'

'But Pebble,' replied Star, 'we're nearly there. The sea is just the other side of this dune and we MUST be near the top. We can't go back now. Your friends are very near – you can hear them when the waves come in. We can't go back now.'

Stroking the pebble gently to stop it trembling, Star stood up and continued to climb, pulling herself up by the bushes which grew in profusion in the soft sand. As she climbed, the voices became louder.

'There's one!' said the first.

'I see it! I got it!' replied the other, followed by the same strange whirring and grinding sound.

By this time the pebble was shaking and rolling its eyes in fright, and Star became worried. Something was seriously wrong with it, and she wondered if she should go back. She had no idea why it had suddenly taken fright so she stopped, undecided, and listened to the waves breaking on the shingle.

'Pebble, what's wrong with you? We're nearly there,' she said, wanting to press on but worried that it was becoming so distressed.

Despite her concern, Star was exasperated. She was in a hurry – she knew she had to get back before her mum found she was missing, and the pebble had told her it wanted to go to the beach to be with its friends – so why was it acting so strangely? The sea was near – just a short distance away – and all she had to do was climb to the top of the dune, go down the other side and they would be there. She decided to ignore the pebble's strange behaviour, and continued climbing the dune.

To her surprise, as she neared the top, she came upon the source of the voices and saw two strange, weather-beaten figures, standing beside an even stranger machine. The machine was made of iron and had big handles, one on each side, something like an old mangle, but with a hole at the top and a little chute at the bottom. The figures were quaint, squarish, made of slabs of a black stone with thin white stripes, and had spindly arms and legs at each corner. Star knew that this was black onyx, a kind of black agate, and as she stared at them in surprise, she couldn't help blurting out, 'You're made of onyx! I saw you in my book!'

'So what if we are,' replied the first figure. 'It's no business of yours.'

'Oh, I'm sorry,' she said, 'I didn't mean to...'

There's one!' interrupted the first figure excitedly, pointing to the ground. 'Grab it!'

'Got it!' said the second, picking up something small and dropping it into the big iron machine.

Together they turned the handles and after a whirring, grinding sound, Star saw a little pile of sand fall out of the chute at the bottom. The second figure took a shovel, lifted the sand and threw it onto the dune which immediately, to Star's surprise, became higher – much higher than she expected from one shovelful of sand!

So that's why the dune keeps getting higher, she thought.

Fascinated, she watched the two figures for a moment and then, feeling the pebble shaking in her pocket and sensing that all was not well, made a move to pass them.

As she did, the first figure, blocked her way, and asked in an unfriendly tone of voice, "Oo are you, then? What yer doin' 'ere, then?'

'I'm Star,' she replied, in as brave a voice as she could manage, 'and I'm going to the beach. It's just the other side...'

'Can't go to the beach,' cut in the first figure, shaking its head, 'not while we're looking fer pebbles.'

'It's our job, see,' replied the second figure, at which the shaking in Star's pocket grew even worse.

'There's one!' said the first figure, suddenly ignoring Star and pointing to the ground. 'Grab it!'

'Got it!' replied the other, followed by the whirring, grinding sound.

Star, who by now was beginning to get very worried, asked anxiously, 'Who are you? What are you doing?'

'We're Sand Makers,' said the first. 'We find pebbles, see, and grind them into sand. It's our job. It's what we do.'

'Someone's got to do it,' grumbled the second and then, noticing something on the ground, excitedly pointed to a small round pebble.

'There's one! Grab it!'

'Got it!' replied the other, dropping the pebble into the machine.

The Sand Makers turned the handles, and after the usual whirring, grinding sound another little pile of sand dropped out of the chute at the bottom of the machine.

This time, as the sand fell out, but before it could be thrown onto the dune, a small greenish figure about the size of a large mouse darted forward and – as quick as a flash – filled a tiny sack with sand and darted off. It all happened so fast that Star almost couldn't believe what she'd seen, but the Sand Makers had evidently seen it before and shook their fists at the little figure, as it scampered off with its sackful of sand.

'Thieving moss agates!' said the first Sand Maker angrily. 'Always stealing our sand.'

'Wretched things,' agreed the second Sand Maker. 'They're so well camouflaged, you can't see them until it's too late.'

'If I ever catch one,' said the first Sand Maker menacingly, 'I know what I'll do with it! I'll turn it into moss agate sand.'

It was just starting to laugh at its little joke, when its attention was distracted by the second Sand Maker, who'd spotted another pebble.

'There's one! Grab it!'

'Got it!' replied the first Sand Maker, picking up the pebble and dropping it into the machine. After looking around to make sure there were no moss agates around, they both turned the handles, and ground the pebble into sand.

*

Undecided what to do next, Star watched the Sand Makers for a moment. The sea was very near, but the Sand Makers were even more grumpy now that their sand had been stolen, and if they wouldn't let her pass before, they were unlikely to let her pass now. The pebble was at the bottom of her pocket, shaking with fright, and she had just made up her mind to go back and find another way, when her thoughts were interrupted by the menacing voice of the first Sand Maker.

'Haven't seen any pebbles round 'ere, 'ave yer? Pebbles is getting very scarce, now. Worth their weight in gold. Yes, very scarce.'

'N... n... no! I haven't seen any pebbles around here, not for ages,' she stammered, suddenly realising the reason for her pebble's terrible fright.

Slowly, she began to back away from the Sand Makers, trying to disguise the pebble by putting her hand in her pocket, but beginning to panic.

You **SURE?**' enquired the second Sand Maker, moving towards her menacingly and staring intently at her smock pocket, 'What's that bulge in yer pocket, then? Looks like a pebble to me.'

'N... No,' replied Star, desperately trying to think of something to say.

'It **IS** a pebble,' cried the first Sand Maker, '**I CAN HEAR ITS TEETH CHATTERING**. Grab it!'

They both lunged at Star, who shrieked, '**NO!**' and turned to run down the sand dune in panic.

The two Sand Makers pursued, shouting, '**SHE'S GOT A PEBBLE! Don't let it get away!**'

Star ran for all she was worth, dodging in and out of the trees and bushes, faster and faster, down and down the steep slope, the soft sand catching at her feet, draining her energy. Frantically, she realised they were gaining on her and the sound of '**GIVE US**

YER PEBBLE' became louder and louder until she almost thought she could feel their breath on her neck. She redoubled her efforts and ran even faster, down and down through the trees and shrubs, her feet dragging in the soft sand, becoming more exhausted than she had ever been in her life. Still she ran, and still the Sand Makers chased her, shouting, **'GIVE US YER PEBBLE!'**

Completely out of breath and feeling she couldn't go any further, Star saw she was near the bottom of the dune, and with the Sand Makers right behind her, made one last great effort. Summoning energy from out of nowhere, she raced for the bottom, but then – *wham!* Her foot caught in the root of a bush and she fell head-over-heels onto the sand, tumbling over and over as she went.

The last thing she saw before lapsing into unconsciousness, was the sight of her pebble – catapulted out of her pocket by the fall – rolling away down the steep slope, squeaking with fright as it went.

*

As she regained her senses, she saw the two Sand Makers standing over her, glaring.

'Give us yer pebble! Hand it over,' said one, hopping from foot to foot in anticipation.

A wave of anger came over Star as she remembered how the Sand Makers had chased her and made her fall, causing her to lose the pebble, and despite being winded and knocked out by the fall, she struggled to her feet.

'HOW DARE YOU!' she shouted, glaring at them.

As she shouted, the Sand Makers, who she now realised were not as big they looked, retreated a few steps and began to look worried. She stamped her foot, and the Sand Makers retreated a few more steps.

'How **DARE** you chase me and make me lose my pebble,' she cried angrily.

'Ah! So yer DID 'ave a pebble,' said the first Sand Maker, nodding at the second and becoming bolder. 'Where is it? Hand it over.'

'I **CAN'T!**' shouted Star. 'It's gone, but if I did have it I wouldn't give it to you because you're **BULLIES!**'

She made a move towards them and the Sand Makers retreated a few more steps, beginning to look even more worried and Star, realising that she now had the upper hand, shouted, '**BULLIES!** What right have you to terrorise defenceless little pebbles? **HOW DARE YOU!**'

With that, she began to chase the Sand Makers back up the dune!

Now frightened in their turn, they ran up the dune, shooting furtive glances at Star and muttering, 'We're only doin' our job. Someone's got to do it.'

Out of breath and still winded by her fall, Star couldn't chase them far, and eventually threw herself down on the sand. She was completely distraught – she'd told the pebble she'd take it back to its friends, and now she'd lost it. As her breath came back she could hear the Sand Makers, high up the dune, collecting more pebbles, having already forgotten all about her.

'There's one! Grab it!'

'Got it!'

Whirr, grind, whirr.

'There's another! Grab it!'

'Got it!'

Whirr, grind, whirr.

Chapter Three

The Old Abandoned Mine

Distraught that the pebble was lost and desperate to find it, Star ran down the dune, searching everywhere, calling, **'PE-BUL, PE-BUL.'** She realised that in the short time she'd known the pebble, she'd become very fond of it, with its wonderful smile, perfect little teeth and innocent, trusting nature. She HAD to find it and take it back to its friends. She'd given her word.

She searched in all the bushes, expecting it to have been snagged as it rolled down, but it was nowhere to be seen. When she came to the bottom of the dune, she realised with dread that she was opposite the entrance to the rock cutting leading to the abandoned mine.

A chill thought struck her. What if the pebble had rolled into the overgrown cutting in front of the mine? She dismissed the thought. Surely, it couldn't have rolled that far? Could it? Surely not, not all the way down the dune, across the overgrown path and into the rock cutting? She searched near the bottom of the dune, and then among the bushes, weeds and brambles on the overgrown path, hoping and expecting that she would find the pebble snagged in a root or bush. She kept calling and listening, and then, with a heavy heart, decided that – somehow – the pebble must have rolled across the path and into the rock cutting.

*

Star parted the bushes and peered into the rock-strewn space leading to the mine entrance, searching for the pebble among the moss-covered rocks, old rails and rusty mine tools outside the forbidding entrance. She searched and searched, but saw nothing, and then called, as loudly as she could, '**PE-BUL**. **PE-BUL**.'

Straining her ears for a reply, all she heard – apart from the sound of dripping water – was a very faint echo, and then silence.

Taking a deep breath, she pushed her way through the screen of trees and bushes into the rock cutting, picking her way over rocks covered with lichens and moss, searching everywhere for the pebble, until she found herself by the old mine truck she had seen earlier, sitting forlornly on its rusty rails.

'**PEBBLE**,' she called. '**Pebble, where are you? Where are you, Pebble?**'

There was no reply, save for a slight echo coming back from somewhere inside the mine, and the eerie sound of dripping water. She looked at the dark, forbidding entrance to the old underground workings and shuddered, but carried on searching, hoping against hope that one of the rocks or old mine tools had stopped the pebble after its headlong flight down the dune.

Having no success, she went back to the sand dune, to the place where she had fallen head-over-heels and seen the pebble rolling away down the slope, tried to work out which way it could have gone and searched to the path at the bottom. Sadly, she returned to the mossy overgrown cutting in front of the mine workings, and began searching again among the old rails, fallen rocks and bits of rusty equipment.

She called again, as loudly as she could, '**PE-BUL. PE-BUL. PE-BUL.**'

Nothing came back but a faint echo from deep inside the mine, and the sound of dripping water. For a while she stood there, wondering what to do.

Suddenly, she heard a voice which made her spirits soar.

'You looking for a pebble?'

Star spun around eagerly, to see that the old Mine Truck was looking at her questioningly.

'You looking for a pebble?' it asked again.

Star, relieved and excited, replied, 'Yes! Oh yes, I am! Have you seen it?'

'Might have,' replied the Mine Truck off-handedly. 'What does it look like?'

'It's a PEBBLE,' she replied, not really knowing what to say. 'You know – a pebble. Oval and flattish. Little ears, nice smile, lovely teeth. You know – a PEBBLE.'

The Mine Truck thought for a while, then asked, 'Does it have legs?'

'NO! It's got arms, but no legs.'

'SEEN IT!' replied the Mine Truck immediately. 'Yep, rolled right past me. Squeaking, it was. I noticed it didn't have no legs.'

Star looked around anxiously.

'Where? Where is it?'

'Rolled right past me,' said the Mine Truck, pointing to the abandoned underground workings. 'It went in there.'

As Star gasped in alarm, the Mine Truck added, with an air of finality, 'You've lost it. It's gone.'

Clutching her head in anguish, Star stared into the dark entrance and shrieked, '**NO! Pebble! Oh NO!**'

'I should forget it,' said the Mine Truck casually. 'Find yourself a new pebble, and...'

Star stopped it in mid-sentence.

'**NO!** I can't forget it. I HAVE to find it. I said I would take it to its friends on the beach. I can't just leave it.' Looking anxiously at the dark overgrown entrance, she said, 'I must find it. I must.'

'Well, you'll HAVE to leave it,' said the Mine Truck, 'because you can't go in there. Forget it, there are plenty of other pebbles. You'll find another one. Perhaps one with legs. Yes, find one with legs,' it chuckled unkindly, 'then you can take it for a walk.'

'I don't WANT another one,' cried Star, 'I want THIS one. I must find it.'

She approached the entrance and stared inside as far as she could see, pushing the dripping ferns aside to get a better look. Although daylight penetrated quite a long way, she found herself staring into a mysterious darkness that really frightened her.

'Don't worry, Pebble,' she said quietly through her tears, 'I'll find you. I will,' and then, quietly and determinedly to herself, 'I WILL. It can't have gone far. Whatever it takes, I WILL find it.'

Star cupped her hands and called into the dark tunnel, as loudly as she could, **'PE-BUL. PE-BUL.'**

She listened desperately for a reply, but apart from the faint echo "PE-BUL, PE-BUL" that came back from deep inside the mine, and the strange sound of dripping water, everything was silent. She called again and listened.

'PE-BUL. PE-BUL.'

There was no reply, and once the echo had died away, just a hushed silence remained, broken only by the steady *drip, drip, drip* of water.

'PEBBLE,' she cried, desperation in her voice. **'WHERE ARE YOU?'** Turning to the Mine Truck, she pleaded, 'How can I find my pebble? Please help me!'

'I can't help you,' replied the Mine Truck. 'Your pebble is inside the mine and you can't go in. Your pebble's lost. Forget it.'

'Why? Why can't I go in?' she cried. 'It can't have gone far. I can find it.'

'You can't go in for lots of reasons,' said the Mine Truck deliberately. 'First, you're only a child...'

Star, interrupting, shouted, '**I'm not! I'm ten!** I'm **NOT** a child. How **DARE** you say that!'

The Mine Truck, ignoring her, went on, 'Secondly, the mine is guarded by two Mine Picks and they are very fierce. They won't let you in. Thirdly, it's very dark in there and you don't have any light, and fourthly there are gemstones in there and they don't take kindly to visitors. They'll keep you there if you go in. If you DID manage to get past the Mine Picks, you'd never get out again.'

Star looked at the Mine Truck defiantly, and said, in a loud and determined voice, 'I DON'T CARE. I have to find my pebble.'

As she turned to look back at the dark, mysterious entrance leading to the abandoned underground workings, the enormity of her task – going into a dark mine without any light, to find a lost pebble – dawned on her, and try as she might, she couldn't stop her tears.

'There you are!' cried the Mine Truck triumphantly. 'You're CRYING! You ARE a child. Forget it. Find another pebble.'

'No!' replied Star, suppressing a sob. 'I said I'd take it to the beach so it can be with its friends, and that is what I'll do. I MUST find it.'

'If you go in there, you'll be in trouble,' said the Mine Truck, emphasising every word. 'The Mine Picks are very fierce and you won't get past them, but even if you did, the gemstones won't let you out again. I wouldn't go in there for ANYTHING – and I'm made of iron! No, you can't go in. Forget it. Find yourself another pebble.'

'There's no such thing as can't,' she replied defiantly. 'I told the pebble I'd take it to the beach to be with its friends, so I'm NOT going to leave it.'

'It's dark in there and the old workings go down a long, long way. If you go in, you won't get out again,' replied the Mine Truck.

'I don't care. I MUST find it,' she cried, 'I can't just abandon it. It's my friend. Could you abandon YOUR friends?'

'Oh yes,' replied the Mine Truck. 'If they went in THERE I would. For sure!'

Star gave the Mine Truck a contemptuous look, then turned again to look into the mine. For a while she stood, peering into the darkness, trying to see if there was any way the pebble could have become snagged close to the entrance.

'Well I'm not abandoning MY friend,' she said deliberately, 'it may be dark and dangerous, but he's in there and I'm going to find him – end of story.'

'Big mistake! Don't say I didn't warn you!' replied the Mine Truck.

Peering through the dripping ferns, she called again, as loudly as she could, '**PE-BUL. PE-BUL. PE-BUL.**'

Listening anxiously for a reply, she heard nothing but the eerie echo, "PE-BUL. PE-BUL. PE-BUL," and the sound of dripping water. Although the mine looked mysterious and frightening, daylight penetrated some way inside and Star could see that the floor was nearly flat and almost dry, with just a little water running out between the rusty rails of the old mine tramway. She called and listened once more.

'**PE-BUL. PE-BUL. PE-BUL.**' But again there was no reply, save for the echo.

Frantically, she searched again among the rocks and rusty tools lying around by the entrance, desperately hoping that she would not be faced with the awful choice of having to go into the mine to search for her pebble, but found nothing. It had disappeared, and Star had to accept that the Mine Truck was right – it HAD rolled into the mine.

For a while she stared into the darkness, wondering what to do, then – bravely, but shivering with fear because this was the most dangerous and frightening thing she had ever done – she made up her mind to go inside the mine to search for the pebble. Summoning up reserves of courage she didn't know she had, she pushed the ferns aside and took one small step into the dark, mysterious tunnel.

The first thing she noticed were the huge number of unusual spiders that had made their homes in the rock walls near the entrance, where daylight still penetrated. Large and spindly, they'd made small webs in the rock crevices, and the daylight reflected in their eyes made them look as if they were sprinkled with tiny jewels. Although Star wasn't fazed by the spiders – she'd never been scared of them – she had no plans to disturb them. Allowing time for her eyes to adjust to the gloom, she took another small step, and then another, and another, all the while searching for the pebble.

The further she went, the darker it became, and she had to keep stopping to let her eyes adjust to the increasing gloom. It was really frightening, and only the thought of the lost pebble stopped her running back into the daylight. Forcing herself to go on, she called, '**PE-BUL. PE-BUL.**'

Once, she thought she heard a reply, but decided it was only the sound of dripping water. Several times she looked back at the entrance and the reassuring sight of daylight, but each time when she turned to look into the darkness again, it took longer for her eyes to adjust, so she gave that up.

The Mine Truck had told her that the mine was guarded by two Mine Picks, and sure enough, she came to a point where, just visible in the dim light, she saw two old picks propped against the tunnel wall. They showed no sign of life, but Star regarded them warily. They looked just like the picks she'd seen on building sites, though a bit more old-fashioned.

She'd just decided that these couldn't be the ones the Mine Truck had told her about, and was about to move on, when suddenly they sprang to life! Before Star had time to blink, they were no longer lying against the wall, but standing in the middle of the tunnel completely blocking her way!

Frightened by the sudden movement, her first instinct was to run away, but something made her stand her ground. There was just enough light to see that they had thin legs and arms and quaint square faces on top of their spindly bodies. They didn't look fierce at all! They actually looked quite comical!

For a while, they glared at her and she stared back, still undecided what to do, but the more she looked the more comical they became. They were supposed to guard the mine and be fierce – so how could they look so comical?

Star's thoughts were racing. It didn't make sense.

She stood her ground, but then began to wonder what would happen if they really WERE fierce. She was still deciding whether to ignore them and carry on searching, or run away, when her thoughts were interrupted by First Pick, who said in a thin screechy voice, which seemed entirely fitting, **'Can't come in.'**

Star had braved the mine and got as far as the picks, so – although still apprehensive – was determined to keep searching for the pebble. Despite her anxiety, she wasn't going to let the Mine Picks stop her now, so in a firm voice replied, 'Please. I must. I have to find my pebble. It rolled in here by mistake. I promised I'd look after it. I must find it. It can't have gone far.'

'Can't,' said First Pick again, shaking its head with an air of finality, its voice sounding like a badly played violin echoing up and down the tunnel.

Star came to the conclusion that they weren't fierce at all, and weren't going to frighten her away – NOT when she had a pebble to find. Gaining confidence, she asked, 'Why not?'

'It's not allowed,' replied First Pick firmly.

'But WHY? Why isn't it allowed? Why can't I go in and find my pebble? It won't take a minute. It rolled in here and can't have gone far,' she replied. 'As soon as I find it, I'll leave.'

'It's just not allowed,' said First Pick, as if reciting from a book.

'So you keep saying,' replied Star. 'But WHY isn't it allowed? WHY can't I just go in to look for my pebble? It can't have gone far. It would only take a minute.'

For a while there was silence, the two picks looking uncomfortable, shifting from one foot to the other. It was clear that First Pick was in charge, but neither seemed to have an answer to Star's question, so she decided that if they couldn't give her a good reason for not going in to look for her pebble, she would ignore them and carry on searching. She was just about to do this when First Pick suddenly blurted out, 'It's **dangerous.** Yes – it's **dangerous!** You can't come in because it's **dangerous**.'

At the word "dangerous" the second pick, which until now hadn't said a word and had been staring straight ahead, swivelled its head 90 degrees to look at First Pick. It stared at it for a few moments, then swivelled its head to the front again, its eyes wide with fright. Staring into the distance for a few more seconds, it swivelled its head sharply to look at First Pick again. 'What do you mean, **dangerous?**' it asked, looking at First Pick intently.

'Yes,' replied First Pick, ignoring Second Pick and still looking at Star, 'it's dangerous. There are bears and tigers in there.'

There was a short silence.

'**BEARS and TIGERS?**' shouted Second Pick, its voice full of anxiety, still looking at First Pick intently. '**You never told me that!**'

There was another silence, during which it swivelled its head to the front, then back to First Pick, and then back to the front again. For a moment it looked straight ahead and then, eyes focussed on the daylight streaming in through the mine entrance, said, **'BEARS AND TIGERS? I'M OFF!'**

Pushing past Star – it ran out of the mine! Star turned to watch its comical legs kicking up puffs of dust as it went, but before she had a chance to realise what was happening, the other pick also took fright and, pushing past Star, ran out of the mine as well – leaving Star alone in the tunnel!

Looking back at the entrance, Star saw the two picks silhouetted in the daylight, and heard them arguing.

'There AREN'T any bears or tigers. I just said that to FRIGHTEN her,' said First Pick.

'Well, it frightened me,' replied Second Pick, firmly.

'How COULD it frighten you? There AREN'T any bears or tigers.'

'You said there WERE,' replied Second Pick.

'We're supposed to guard the mine. I said that to frighten her. Let's go back in.'

'NOT if there are bears and tigers in there,' replied Second Pick, with an air of finality.

'There AREN'T any bears or tigers in there,' responded First Pick in exasperation.

'You said there WERE!' replied Second Pick. 'If there AREN'T any bears or tigers, why did you run out after me? YOU MUST HAVE SEEN ONE.'

'How could I have seen one?' responded First Pick. 'There AREN'T any to see.'

'But you said there WERE,' replied Second Pick.

At this, First Pick lost its patience and presence of mind. Very deliberately, clipping Second Pick on the ear with each syllable – it shouted, 'There **AREN'T** any bears... there **AREN'T** any tigers... I only said that to **SCARE** her.'

'Well, it scared me,' replied Second Pick, at which the argument turned into a fight.

Framed at the entrance, arguing and scuffling, Star couldn't help smiling as she heard their voices, echoing down the tunnel.

'There are NO bears…'

'But you said…'

'NO tigers…'

'But you said…'

*

The antics of the Mine Picks had given Star the confidence to go on searching for the pebble, at least as far as the daylight would allow, but she shivered as she turned to look again into the dark, mysterious tunnel, the walls dripping with water and the tiny spiders' eyes watching her every move.

She hesitated, then eased her way along the tunnel, allowing her eyes to adjust as she went, searching and calling loudly for the pebble, **'PE-BUL. PE-BUL. PE-BUL.'**

There was no answer, and all she heard was the echo, louder now that she was deeper inside the mine, and the sound of the water dripping from the roof, amplified and distorted by the acoustics inside the tunnel. She went as far as she could, searching and calling, without any sight or sound of the pebble, and when it was too dark to go any further, she stopped, held her head in her hands, and began to cry.

'Pebble,' she sobbed. 'You were so trusting, and you had such a lovely smile. I've let you down. Now you will never get to see your friends again. I can't bear the thought of you being in this dark place forever.'

For a while, the tears of regret flowed freely. Feeling lost and wishing more than ever that her dad was there, she looked into the darkness one last time, listening to the silence and the eerie sound of dripping water. With one last effort, she called as loudly as she could into the impenetrable darkness, her lungs almost bursting with the effort.

'**PE-BUL. PE-BUL. PE-BUL.**' She listened as the echo died away, until all that remained was the sound of dripping water, and her quiet sobbing. For a long time she stood, head down, missing her dad and her new friend, as miserable as she had ever felt in her entire life. She let the tears flow freely, knowing that – although she had done all that she could – it just wasn't enough.

With a heavy heart, Star looked towards the daylight flooding through the entrance to the old mine workings and began to make her way back along the tunnel. Leaving the pebble, after promising to take it to the beach to be with its friends, was one of the most difficult things she had ever had to do. She hated breaking her promise.

Suddenly, she stopped. Was the tunnel playing tricks on her? She listened to the silence, decided it was, and was just about to move on when she heard it again! This time, there was no mistake, and her spirits soared!

'HELP!'

Star spun around, and listened intently.

'HELP!' came the voice again, weak and far off. 'HELP!'

'PEBBLE! PEBBLE!' she shouted excitedly, **'Pebble, where are you?'**

'I'm here,' came a weak voice from out of the darkness, deep inside the mine. 'I'm here, in a puddle.'

'PEBBLE!' shouted Star. **'DON'T MOVE. I'm coming! Splash your arms so I can hear you. It's too dark for me to see.'**

Star heard a weak *splash, splash, splash* coming from the darkness, far beyond where she could see. With a happy heart, she began to edge her way further into the mine, her outstretched hand using one wall as a guide.

'I'm coming, Pebble!' she shouted. **'Don't move!'**

'I can't move. I haven't got any legs and I can't swim!' came the faint reply.

Star smiled, and finally reached the sound of splashing. To her unspeakable delight there, in a puddle of water, grinning up at her with his white teeth shining in the gloom – was the pebble!

Picking it up tenderly, Star gave it an affectionate hug.

'PEBBLE! I was so worried! I thought you were lost forever!' Relieved and happy, but pretending to be cross, she said, 'And here you were all the time, having a bath!'

She dried the little pebble on her handkerchief, and with an overwhelming sense of relief, smiled at it, seeing the flash of brilliant white teeth as it smiled back, lighting up the tunnel.

'Thank you for rescuing me,' it said. 'It was very brave of you to come in here. When I rolled down the hill I was going so fast I couldn't stop and then I rolled in here. I thought I'd have to spend the rest of my life in this dark tunnel, and I'd never see you or my friends again.'

Star laughed, with a mixture of relief, happiness and pride – against all the odds, she had found and rescued the pebble!

'The sooner we get out of this horrible place, Pebble, the better, and then I'll take you to the beach to be with your friends,' she said with feeling.

'Ooooh. I can't wait!' it replied, giving Star a memorable smile.

'Well, no more falling out of my pocket!' said Star, more severely than she meant. 'From now on I'm going to hold you tightly, and we won't go near those Sand Makers again. We won't take any more chances – we'll go back to the signpost and go the other way.'

Giving the pebble another tender hug, Star placed it gently in her smock pocket, where it took up its usual position, peering out like a baby kangaroo. She turned towards the entrance, and in a confident and happy voice said, 'Let's go, Pebble!'

Working her way towards the daylight streaming in through the entrance, using one hand to steady herself against the tunnel wall, she could still see the two Mine Picks arguing, and as she neared the entrance – and safety – she heard their voices echoing down the tunnel.

'NO bears and NO tigers…'

'But you SAID there were…'

'ONLY to frighten HER. How many times must I tell you? There AREN'T any bears or tigers.'

'Why did you run out after me then? You must have SEEN one.'

'How could I see one when there AREN'T ANY to see?'

'You said there WERE… If you didn't see one, you must have smelt one.'

'I didn't SEE one and I didn't SMELL one.'

'You HEARD one, then… Why else would you run out after me?'

Beyond the Mine Picks, it was still a bright sunny day and with a light heart, delighted to have found her pebble, Star made her way towards the entrance. As the daylight drew nearer, the going became easier and she was sure she'd now be able to put the pebble on the beach and get home before she was missed.

'We'll soon be out of here, Pebble,' she said.

She spoke too soon!

Chapter Four

A Desperate Situation

'**STOP!**'

Star froze at the pebble's urgent command.

Before she had time to ask why, there came a deep rumbling which reverberated through the mine workings like rolling thunder, shaking the ground beneath her feet. Gasping in alarm, she reached out to the tunnel wall for support and for a moment, shocked by this new development, leaned against the wall, eyes fixed on the mine entrance and safety, unable to move.

As the rumbling echoed through the mine, both Mine Picks stopped arguing, cast anxious glances into the tunnel and ran away, and Star instinctively reached into her pocket to comfort the pebble. She knew she had to reach daylight before something really bad happened, and with the rumbling still reverberating through the tunnel, made up her mind to run – but before she could, the ground began shaking and swaying, as if giant ocean waves were rippling through the earth. The rumbling came back, this time like the worst thunder she could imagine, and Star was thrown to her knees, all the while staring at the daylight, determined to make her escape at the first opportunity.

The shaking and swaying became more violent, and she was thrown against one wall and then the other. Despite trying to focus on the daylight at the entrance, eventually she became disorientated, and in the end all she could do was try to protect herself and hope that the tremors and echoing thunder would soon end, allowing her to dash to safety.

At one point the swaying lessened and she was able to stand up, but almost immediately was forced back to her knees as the tunnel floor shook with even more powerful vibrations. Despite her ordeal, and the panic that was beginning to overtake her, Star knew that she had to get out and whenever the swaying eased she would struggle up, only to be thrown down again moments later. The entrance was so near, but it was impossible to run or even walk while the ground was shaking so violently.

Then, with a feeling of despair, she watched as a boulder fell from the roof of the tunnel and smashed into the ground, followed by another and then another. Overwhelmed by the shaking and the terror of seeing rocks and boulders crashing down to block the entrance, she held the pebble tightly, trying to fight off the panic that was engulfing her, desperately wishing it would all go away.

Horrified, she watched as more rocks and boulders crashed down, until finally all she could see was a tiny patch of daylight through a small gap at the very top.

As the violent trembling and shaking began to subside, she stared, mesmerised, at this tiny patch of light – wonderful, wonderful daylight. Then another rock crashed down, and in an instant it was gone, snuffed out forever.

It was the last daylight Star was to see for a very long time.

*

As the last of the boulders crashed to the ground, completely blocking the tunnel, an inky blackness descended and Star was engulfed in a darkness so complete, so utterly devoid of light that she thought she was blind. In abject despair, she found herself stroking the pebble and holding its tiny hand. Numb with fright, she found this contact with her little companion very comforting.

The truth was, she was trapped inside an old mine by a huge fall of rocks, and there was no way out. Her mother had no idea where she was and she had no light. Feeling completely lost, and thinking she was blind in the total darkness, Star thought her life had come to an end – or was about to – and wished more than ever that her dad was there to tell her what to do.

As she spiralled down into total despair, a strange thing happened.

From out of the darkness, she heard a calm, authoritative and reassuring voice. It was the pebble.

'Star – please may I call you Star? I heard you tell the Sand Makers your name was Star. It's a nice name. Do you mind if I call you Star?'

She was too distraught to answer, though in the darkness she nodded.

Calmly, the pebble went on, 'You were very brave. You came to rescue me, a little pebble, and that took real courage, so one way or another, I'm going to make sure we get out, so you can go home.'

'But Pebble,' she replied, hysterically, 'I can't see. I'm blind. The rocks have blocked the only way out. How can we EVER get out now?'

Panicking at the thought of her own disappearance – just like her dad – and overwhelmed by grief at the way it would distress her mum, Star began to sob hysterically.

The pebble's comforting voice broke through her misery, and brought her back.

'Star! May I call you Star?'

'Of course, Pebble,' she replied through her tears, 'but what about you? Do you have a name?'

'Well,' replied the pebble, 'I'm made of a kind of jasper, but I don't think I have a na...'

'Jasper!' cut in Star, between sobs. 'That's a name. I'll call you Jasper. Jasper Pebble.'

Star couldn't see it, but the pebble was smiling, pleased with his new name.

'Thank you, Star! We may be trapped now, but we'll get out – you'll see!'

Star could feel that her new friend was excited, because he always tugged at her pocket when he had something important to say, and sure enough, his excited voice cut through the darkness.

'Star! I KNOW there must be another way out.'

Still overwrought, but comforted by her little friend's calm voice, she replied, 'Yes, Peb... er... Jasper, but how do you KNOW that? The tunnel is blocked. I can't move the stones and I can't see. How can there be another way out?'

Her voice trailed off to a whisper, full of misery.

'Do you remember,' came Jasper's excited voice, 'when we were outside, and saw the mine for the first time?'

'Yes,' she sobbed, hesitantly.

'Well, didn't we feel a breeze coming out of the mine? Strong enough to waggle my ears?'

'Yes,' she replied, not sure where this was leading.

From the darkness came the triumphant voice of her little friend.

'Well, Star, it stands to reason! If the wind was coming out there, it must be going in somewhere else. Don't you see? There must be ANOTHER entrance! There must be another way out! We just have to find it and then we can go home! We're NOT trapped!'

For the first time since the tunnel collapsed in the awful chaos of noise and dust, Star's spirits began to rise. Jasper, who before the disaster had just been an endearing little pebble with a lovely smile who wanted to go back to the beach, was now becoming something quite different – a tower of strength, support and comfort!

'**JASPER!**' she cried. 'Another way out? But where? Where is it? And how will we find it when I'm blind? Can you see in the dark?'

Star couldn't see it, but Jasper shook his head. He couldn't see in the dark either.

She lapsed into despair again as the enormity of their problem hit her. How could they find their way out in complete darkness, without a light? It just wasn't possible.

'Jasper,' she wailed, 'this could be a labyrinth. The tunnel could go on for miles. There's no way we can find our way out in the dark. I can't even tell which way the tunnel is any more. I can't see to move even an inch. I think I'm blind.'

Huge sobs racked her body and she sank into a deep sense of hopelessness. She was trapped, and she couldn't see. She would never see her mum again and as for supper – well, she would never have supper again. Her life would soon be over, without anyone ever knowing what had happened to her. She would have disappeared off the face of the earth, just like her dad. How could her life NOT end, trapped like this in an abandoned mine?

Overwhelmed by these thoughts, and how it would affect her mum, Star felt her chest begin to constrict and her breath become shallow and difficult. Panic was beginning to engulf her and she was about to give up, but Jasper, sensed this.

'Star?'

'Yes, Jasper?' she replied quietly, trying to overcome the emotions that were overwhelming her.

'Did you know that there was once going to be a sports day – a kind of competition – held on the beach by your house?'

Taken aback by Jasper's question, which came out of the blue and seemed completely out of context with their situation, Star was too miserable to reply, but Jasper went on,

'Yes, but they had to cancel it.'

'Why was that?' Star managed to ask, still on the verge of hysteria.

'Well, when it came to the first race, they lined up all the pebbles and then discovered that none of them had any legs and couldn't run...'

For a moment there was silence, as Star took in what Jasper was saying, but then, unable to stop herself, she burst out laughing. The incongruity of being trapped in an abandoned mine, unable to see, with a little pebble without legs telling jokes about other pebbles without legs, was just too much, and Star laughed and laughed, completely unable to stop. The tension that had been about to overwhelm her began to ebb away.

Jasper was shaking with laughter too, and as Star and Jasper, lost in the inky blackness of the old mine tunnel, laughed at Jasper's little joke, she began to regain her senses. She realised that Jasper must have been just as frightened as she was when the mine collapsed, and gratitude for the little pebble welled up inside her. In the darkness she felt for her friend, and was comforted when his little hand grasped hers.

*

For a while she leaned against the tunnel wall, stroking Jasper tenderly, thinking about their situation. True – as Jasper had said – there might be another way out of the mine, but how could they possibly find it in the dark? Without a light, everything was pitch black and she would be reduced to crawling on all fours, with only her sense of touch to guide her. The mine might go on for miles, and she could easily spend the rest of her days – until she starved – crawling around in the darkness, not knowing where she was. It was an impossible situation.

But then – what about Jasper? He had changed from an ordinary sea pebble into something quite special. Okay, he still didn't have any legs, but his sensitivity was something you'd never expect from a pebble. To tell her a joke about a sports day having to be cancelled because none of the pebbles had legs was a stroke of genius! She smiled again at the thought of the organisers lining up the pebbles, then finding they had no legs, and running around like headless chickens before cancelling the games. Despite their impossible situation, she began to feel better!

'That was good, Jasper!' she said, looking down in the darkness to where she thought Jasper would be.

She noticed the quick flash of Jasper's brilliant white teeth.

'What am I doing, Star?' came Jasper's calm voice.

'You're making me laugh, Jasper. Thank you for making me laugh. I feel better.'

'No, Star – what am I doing NOW, at this very moment?'

'You're smiling, Jasper. I can see your tee… **TEETH! JASPER, I CAN SEE YOUR TEETH!'**

It was true! Very dimly, Star could see the brilliant white of Jasper's little teeth shining through the darkness! She wasn't blind after all! Somehow – somehow – she could see! But – how?

'JASPER!' she gasped, amazement and disbelief in her voice. 'I can SEE! I'm not blind. What's happening?'

Jasper's reassuring voice came out of the darkness, trembling with excitement.

'Star, turn around! Turn around and look behind you. Look down the tunnel.'

Taking a deep breath, Star turned and looked down the inky-black tunnel.

The sight that met her eyes took her breath away!

It had been transformed! Completely transformed! What had been a dark, forbidding, mysterious mine tunnel was now a wonderland of unimaginable beauty. From within the rock walls, shining with a soft luminescence, were thousands upon thousands of tiny crystals, fluorescing in every possible colour, giving a magical light which danced and twinkled along the walls and roof of the tunnel, just like the display of the Northern Lights Star had seen when her parents took her to visit Lapland one Christmas when she was young.

For a while she gazed at the wonderful sight, forgetting even that she was trapped inside the mine and had nearly been crushed by a fall of rocks. All her worries – which moments before had overwhelmed her – now seemed to be soothed by this wonderful, shimmering light.

'Jasper!' she exclaimed after a while. 'Have you ever seen ANYTHING so beautiful? What has happened? We can see again!'

'Star, some crystals in the rocks are fluorescing. I think they have always been there, but we couldn't see them until our eyes got used to the dark. They seem bright to us, but probably they're not that bright at all. We wouldn't see them unless everything else was so dark. I've seen some wonderful things in my time, in different oceans and seas, but this is the most beautiful thing I've ever seen.'

Lost for words, Star found herself stroking Jasper tenderly as she gazed in awe at the magical tunnel – no longer mysterious and frightening – as it twisted and turned, gently snaking its way down into the earth.

*

For a while, Star continued to gaze at the enchanting sight, her despair now replaced by a strange feeling of optimism, but then the cold wind of reality made her reflect on what had happened. First of all, she had nearly been crushed to death by a fall of rocks which had trapped her inside the abandoned mine, but then Jasper (how clever he was!) had deduced that there must be another way out, and then her biggest fear – that she was blind or couldn't move because it was too dark to see – had been removed when she saw the wonderful crystal lights fluorescing, lighting up the tunnel. She had to face the fact that she was still trapped inside the mine, with no way of knowing how long it would take to find another way out – if there was one. Her big consolation was Jasper – clever, comforting Jasper – who was now her sole companion.

As these thoughts went through her mind, she came to the conclusion that it was now up to her to save them both, and for that she needed to remain strong. Whatever the future might bring, and however difficult it might be, Star knew that she would have to be resolute. The more she thought about it, the more determined she became to overcome whatever dangers lay ahead, and the stronger she felt. Somehow, she could sense her dad encouraging her.

'Jasper,' she said after a while, 'thank you for cheering me up. I was very close to going under after the tunnel collapsed, but you saved me. I really think we WILL find a way out. We're a team now, and when we get out, I WILL take you to your friends on the beach. That's a promise.'

Jasper smiled, and the whole tunnel seemed to brighten.

'Do you know what we need, Jasper?' she asked, forcing herself to sound cheerful.

'No, Star? What?'

'We need – a PLAN! We can't stay here forever. We need to make a plan which will get us out of here, so you can get to the beach and I can get home before my mum finds I'm gone.'

'Right,' said Jasper, in a very business-like manner. 'We'll make a plan!'

As Star was trying to think what to do for the best, she felt his little hand grasp her own, and he looked up contritely.

'Star, I'm so sorry this has happened. This only happened because you came in to rescue me. It's all my fault. I wish I'd stayed asleep forever,' he said, his voice trailing off miserably.

'Jasper!' replied Star tenderly. 'How can you SAY that? It wasn't your fault that you rolled in here, and the very least I could do was try to find you. How could I possibly NOT rescue you when I said I'd take you to live with your friends? I was very happy to do it.'

'You were so brave,' he replied, 'I could never imagine such bravery. I know you were terrified to come in here, and…'

'Shush, Jasper,' Star responded tenderly, 'we're a team now. We'll find a way out and then everything will be fine. I'll get you to the beach, and I'll go home to my mum.'

She nearly added 'to face the music' but didn't, in case it upset her little friend.

At the thought of her mum, Star gave an involuntary sob. She missed her mum, and regretted the harsh words she'd said. She began to appreciate all the wonderful things her mum had done for her, despite her sadness at losing her husband. Star made a promise to herself that – if she ever got home – things would be different.

Putting those thoughts aside, and forcing herself to be positive, she said, 'We need to make a plan, but first let's just see if there's any way we can get past the rocks that are blocking our way.'

She turned to look at the chaotic fall of rocks and boulders, but although they didn't look unkind, they had their arms folded and were shaking their heads in a way that brooked no argument. They really were trapped.

'Jasper,' she said quietly, 'I don't think these rocks will let us pass,' at which they shook their heads, 'and they seem too big to move,' at which they smiled and nodded. 'So we have to think of something else. We know, thanks to your brilliant deduction, that there should be another way out. We can't go past the rocks,' she glanced at them again, to see that they were still shaking their heads, 'so the only thing we can do is go down the tunnel and see if we can find it. What do you think?'

'I agree. Now that we can see where we're going, it should be easy,' he replied, sounding optimistic.

She looked affectionately at the little pebble, nestling in her pocket.

'The best thing, Jasper, is that we're both safe,' she said, 'but I'm not letting you out of my sight again! We're a team, and we'll stick together now through thick and thin! And no more falling out of my pocket!'

Jasper smiled, a happy, warm smile, which lifted Star's spirits.

'Yes – a TEAM!' he said, proudly.

'Come on,' she said, standing up and making sure Jasper was safe and secure in her pocket, 'I feel we're going to get out of here! Let's go!'

Tentatively, she began to make her way along the tunnel, walking between the rusty rails of the old tramway, with Jasper peering out of her pocket, fascinated by the warm glow of the thousands of tiny fluorescing crystals that were now lighting their way.

'Aren't they gorgeous?' she remarked, looking at the fluorescing crystals. 'They're like tiny little light bulbs, but in all different colours.'

'Amazing,' he replied. 'I've seen fluorescence in the sea before, but that's usually green. These are shimmering in every colour you can imagine. I've never seen anything like it.'

Mindful that she needed to find a way out of the mine before she was missed, Star quickened her pace, and soon the fall of rocks which had trapped them so spectacularly was left behind. When she glanced back, she was relieved that she couldn't see it anymore, because it reminded her of the very narrow escape they'd had. If Jasper – with his amazing hearing – hadn't cried "**stop**" when he did, she would have been crushed, and that would have been the end.

Jasper, keeping a good lookout, suddenly tugged at her pocket, and she stopped abruptly.

'What is it?' Star asked anxiously.

'The lights. They're going out.'

'WHAT?' she exclaimed, her heart sinking fast.

She already had an uneasy feeling that something was wrong, but hadn't been able to put her finger on it. Now that Jasper mentioned it, it was obvious. The tunnel, which stretched away into the distance, was – slowly and imperceptibly – getting darker.

She stared ahead, and saw that the tramway rails disappeared into darkness.

'Jasper, what's happening?' she asked, her voice rising in panic.

Having been plunged into pitch darkness when the mine collapsed, then seeing the tiny crystals fluorescing, the thought of being plunged back into darkness again was too much to bear, and her panic came flooding back.

'Jasper,' she cried, 'what are we going to do?'

On hearing Jasper's calm voice, she felt her panic begin to subside.

'THIS tunnel is getting dark, Star – but look! There's a patch of light shining on the wall further on. I bet that's coming from a different tunnel.'

And it was! Star walked quickly towards the patch of light and saw that Jasper was right. The light shining on the wall was coming from the entrance to a new, brightly lit tunnel which Star hadn't seen because of a slight bend up ahead, but Jasper, with his acute eyesight and brilliant power of deduction, had seen the light shining on the wall and come to the right conclusion.

The new tunnel branched off to the right at 90 degrees, and was completely different. The tunnel they had been following was a typical old mine tunnel with the remains of a tramway. The new tunnel was much more regular and even, and looked just like the type of corridor you would find in a building, except that it was cut through solid rock. More importantly, it was brightly lit and shimmered with colour.

At first sight, it seemed to be the answer and Star's hopes rose, but as she looked into the new tunnel, she became anxious again. What if it led them to the gemstones? The Mine Truck had told her that if she went into the mine, the gemstones wouldn't let her out again.

'Jasper,' she said anxiously, 'I was told there were gemstones down here, and if they caught me they wouldn't let me out. I'm worried this new tunnel could lead to where the gemstones live. If so, we'll have to forget it – it's too risky.'

Jasper, peering down the new passage and then the old, gave his conclusion. 'It probably IS where the gemstones live, Star, but without any light we have no choice.'

His voice became quieter.

'The problem is, the old tunnel may lead us back to the surface, but it's dark and without any light we can't go that way. The new tunnel may lead us away from the surface, and take us to where the gemstones are, but it's well lit – so it's the only way we can go whether we like it or not.'

Star had already thought of the possibility that the old tunnel would lead them back to the surface whereas the new one wouldn't, and was loathe to abandon it. In her heart, she knew that it would be futile to try and follow the old miners' tunnel without any light, even if it did lead to a way out, but was worried sick that the new tunnel would – if the Mine Truck was right – end up with her being imprisoned forever in this underground world.

'Maybe we should carry on as far as we can, Jasper,' she said anxiously. 'You never know, maybe there will be more light up ahead and we may find a way out quite soon.'

'We could,' he replied, 'and I have an idea that might help. Why don't we see if there is a breeze coming along the tunnel? If there is, that might tell us if it's worth following.'

'Great idea, Jasper!' said Star, grasping at any straw, and marvelling at her little friend's powers of reason.

'Let's go as far as we can,' he replied, 'and see if there's a wind coming down the tunnel. If there is, that means it could lead to another way out, and then we'll have to decide what to do.'

'Okay. Hold tight little friend,' she said, as she began to make her way down the ever-darkening tunnel.

*

From time to time Star turned to look back at the bright light shining on the wall, coming out of the new passage, and wondered if she was doing the right thing. Even if there WAS a breeze, how would they be able to follow a completely dark tunnel? And what if the Mine Truck had been wrong about the gemstones? It had been wrong about the Mine Picks – they weren't fierce at all. Perhaps the gemstones would be friendly, and even show her the way to go home.

Slowly, they made their way into the increasing gloom. Finally it became too dark to see, and Star had to stop and lean against the tunnel wall for support. She listened to the silence, disturbed only by the sound of her pounding heart, and tried to feel if there was any kind of a breeze on her face.

'Can you feel anything, Jasper?' she asked anxiously. 'I can't.'

Jasper's answer was final.

'No, Star, nothing. I don't think this leads back to the surface.'

'If the tunnel is blocked, would we still feel a breeze? If the wind can't get out, surely it wouldn't be able to go in either? Could that be why there's no breeze?'

'I thought of that,' he said, 'but it all comes down to this. We don't have a light and we can't see in the dark, so we CAN'T go this way.'

Jasper was right, and Star knew it. Without some sort of light, it would be impossible to carry on. They would HAVE to go back and try the new tunnel, whatever the dangers. At least they would be able to see where they were going.

'We'll have to go back, then,' she replied, disappointment in her voice, 'and try the other way. You're right, Jasper. We have no choice.'

Slowly, she retraced her steps to where the new tunnel branched off, and then stopped. It was warm, brightly lit and – she had to admit – did look inviting, but still she hesitated. The Mine Truck had been quite specific. If she went in she wouldn't be allowed out again. With a voice full of anxiety she said, 'Jasper, when you were lost inside the mine, and I was outside looking for you, I saw a Mine Truck who told me that there were gemstones in here, and if they caught me they would never let me out again. If we go down this tunnel and we meet some gemstones... what if they capture us? What if they try to keep us here forever?'

The thought that she might never see her mum or her friends again overwhelmed her.

'Jasper,' she sobbed, 'what can we do? I'm so frightened. I may never be able to go home. I might have to stay here forever.'

As she put her hand down to stroke him she felt his little hand grasp hers, and then heard his gentle, reassuring voice.

'I won't let them hurt you, Star. The gemstones won't be angry once they know you only came here to rescue me. After all, I'm a stone just like they are, and I'll tell them the truth! I'll keep you safe.'

He gave Star's hand a comforting squeeze and one of his lovely smiles and immediately she began to feel better.

'Thank you, Jasper,' she said, feeling more positive again.

Jasper smiled, another of his award-winning smiles.

'You came here to rescue me, Star – and I'll rescue you back! We're a TEAM! Now, let's make another plan!'

Star, who had now recovered enough to think the matter through, said, 'Jasper, I don't know what I'd do without you. I am amazed how clever you are!'

He smiled again, this time with pride, and went on, 'Thank you, Star. As for our plan, we need light to see where we're going – even I can't see in the dark – so we have to go down this new tunnel whether we like it or not, then face up to whatever we find. Let's go down carefully, so we're not surprised. I'll listen out. I've got very good hearing and...'

'I know!' interrupted Star. 'You've got such tiny ears, but your hearing is amazing. You saved my life when the rocks began to fall. You heard them long before I did and if you hadn't warned me, I wouldn't be here now.'

'I was glad I heard them, but as I was saying, if you stop every so often, I'll listen out. If we meet anything, I should hear it before it sees us.'

'Brilliant!' she said admiringly, having forgotten how upset she had been just moments before.

'Let's go, then,' he said, tugging at Star's pocket and smiling, taking up his usual position, and peering out to see where they were going.

Star smiled at the little pebble, and after stroking him affectionately for a moment, took a deep breath – and stepped inside.

Chapter Five

The Only Way Home

The new tunnel, about as wide as a school corridor, had a flat smooth floor and it sloped gently downwards, snaking its way along. Whenever they came to a bend, Star took extra care, stopping to let Jasper listen before peering around. When he listened, he would cup one tiny hand behind his ear, which made her smile because he looked so earnest when he did this. It all seemed so conspiratorial, and if the situation hadn't been so serious, she would have regarded creeping along the tunnel – trying not to be seen – as an exciting adventure.

They went on like this for what seemed a long time, with Star making frequent stops for Jasper to listen, and during one of these, she felt a tug at her pocket and heard Jasper's urgent whisper, 'Star! I can hear something!'

Without thinking, she flattened herself against the wall.

'What is it?' she whispered, her heart beating

faster. 'What did you hear?'

He looked up with a puzzled look.

'I can't make it out. It's a kind of scratching. A cross between a scratching and a squeaking. It comes and goes. I'm not sure what it is.'

Star listened, but could hear nothing except the deep silence and her pounding heart.

'Are you sure you heard something?' she asked. 'I can't hear anything.'

'Yes, it was definitely a scratching. It comes and goes.'

'Does it sound like an animal?' she asked anxiously.

'Not really,' he replied. 'I don't know what it can be.'

'Does it sound dangerous?'

'I don't think so,' he replied, and then, after listening some more, 'whatever it is, it's quite small and it doesn't sound dangerous. It might even be smaller than me, but we still need to be careful.'

'My word, Jasper,' she said affectionately, looking down at the little pebble with his hand cupped to his ear, 'you really do have amazing hearing! I can't hear a thing! What shall we do?'

'Let's go on,' he replied, 'but until we know what's causing the scratching, we must keep to the edge and be especially careful. If we come to a bend, let me look around first. I'm smaller and maybe they won't see me.'

Presently she too could hear the sound of scratching and squeaking, coming from somewhere around a bend. She couldn't figure it out either. It sounded like someone writing with very bad chalk on a scratchy blackboard, but knew it couldn't be that. Perhaps it was a mouse, or even some animal she'd never seen before. A new species, perhaps – with big teeth – and hungry!

'I can hear it now, Jasper,' she whispered.

She listened some more, and decided that it might be a mouse.

'It sounds like a mouse to me,' she said, adding timidly, 'I don't like mice. What do you think? Shall we go on?'

'We need to see what it is, so we can ask how to get out of here,' he whispered. 'Tiptoe up to the bend, as quietly as you can, and hold me out at arm's length so I can peep around the corner.'

Star was worried. She wanted Jasper to stay in her pocket for safety, but couldn't think of a better idea, so agreed to his suggestion. Carefully, she tiptoed up to the bend, and pressing herself against the wall, edged her way around as far as she could. The scratching was still there.

What COULD it be? It sounded like a mouse, or even a rat! But what would they be doing down here anyway? Or a cat? A horrible thought struck her! If it was a cat, could it be a BIG cat… like a TIGER? *The Mine Pick had said there were tigers and bears down here, and if it IS a tiger*, she thought, *it might be hungry*. What if it regarded her as a snack…?

Star dismissed the thought. The Mine Pick had told her there were bears and tigers only to frighten her. No, it had to be a mouse. If it was bigger than a mouse, surely the noise would be louder? The noise did seem loud, but only because the rest of the tunnel was so quiet.

The suspense was awful, and for a moment the fear of the unknown made anything seem possible. Perhaps it was an elephant?

Fighting an urge to run back the way they'd come, she whispered to Jasper, 'Shall we go on?'

His whispered reply came back swiftly. 'Yes!'

'Okay,' she answered, regaining her sense of proportion as she realised that an elephant wouldn't fit inside the tunnel, 'I'll hold you out as far as I can, so you can see around the corner.'

For a moment she listened to the scratching, but then, having made her decision, took Jasper out of her pocket, held him as tightly as she could in her right hand – her tennis hand, which she thought would be stronger – and flattened herself against the wall. Taking a deep breath, she closed her eyes and pushed Jasper out as far as he would go.

The tension was unbearable, and Star was just wondering if she could cope with the strain of anticipation and the difficulty of holding Jasper at arm's length, when the silence was broken by Jasper's urgent whisper. 'STAR! STAR! Wrong way!'

'What do you mean?' she whispered, unable to understand what he was saying.

'WRONG WAY,' came Jasper's urgent response, still whispered, but getting louder.

Star was puzzled.

'This is the ONLY way, Jasper,' she said. 'What do

you mean? Have we come down the wrong tunnel?'

Jasper, now sounding frantic and a bit hysterical, replied, **'No, Star. I'm the WRONG WAY!'**

'Jasper, never mind that, can you SEE anything?' she asked anxiously, her arm beginning to tremble from the strain of holding him out so far.

By now, the tension was almost too much to bear and Star began to panic.

'NO!' he replied, his whisper turning almost into a shout. **'I'M FACING THE WRONG WAY**. I can't see anything. Pull me back, quick.'

Star quickly pulled her arm back. When she opened her eyes and saw the panicked expression on Jasper's little face, she burst out laughing.

She'd pushed Jasper around the bend the wrong way round, with his eyes facing backwards!

In an instant, the tension that had been building to breaking point disappeared in a flurry of hysterics! Laughing, but trying not to make a sound, Star leaned against the tunnel wall and shook uncontrollably, tears rolling down her face. Jasper – back to front! His little eyes peering backwards! It was just so funny! And the anxious look on his face as she pulled him back was priceless!

Jasper, caught up in the mood, began to laugh as well. The more he laughed, the more she laughed, and the more Star laughed, the more he laughed, and when one stopped, it didn't take much to set them both off again. Eventually, they subsided into a series of giggles, but when Jasper gasped, 'Next time, Star...' they both burst out laughing again.

Eventually, all the tension was gone and Star slid down the wall and sat with her back to it, holding Jasper with both hands and smiling at him from time to time. The scratching had stopped as soon as they had begun to laugh, so whatever it was – she thought – must have heard them and run away. She remembered that this kind of uncontrollable laughter had happened once before, when she had been helping her aunt do the dishes one day. They had found her uncle's teeth on the plate, and this had set them off giggling – but when her uncle came in and said, 'Hath anyone theen my theeth?' it sent them into hysterics. And when he said, 'Ith not funny,' they couldn't control themselves and had ended up rolling about on the floor, unable to speak.

The thought set her off again, which set Jasper off, and they laughed so much she had to gasp for air, and poor Jasper was completely wet with tears.

Eventually, having regained her composure, she whispered, 'Jasper?'

'Yes, Star?'

'The scratching has stopped. Whatever it was must have heard us and run away.'

After their fit of laughter Star was feeling better, and pulling herself together, said, 'We must get on, otherwise we'll be here forever. Come on, let's see what's around the bend.'

Holding Jasper in her right hand, this time making sure he was facing the right way, she braced herself against the wall, took a deep breath and pushed him around the corner, trying not to laugh.

'Can you see anything?' she whispered.

'No,' came his whispered reply. 'You need to push me further around.'

Star edged herself further around the bend, pushing Jasper further and further around the corner. Again, the suspense was unbearable.

'See anything yet?' she whispered anxiously.

Expecting to hear his whispered reply, Star heard instead a rich warm voice that reminded her of her favourite aunt.

'Ah! Visitors! Please do come in!'

She jumped in alarm and dropped Jasper, who – still wet from his tears – had slipped out of her outstretched hand and crashed onto the hard rock floor. He bounced once, and with a muffled 'Ouch,' began to roll away down the gently sloping tunnel.

Thoroughly annoyed at having dropped her little friend, Star shrieked and dashed forward to pick him up, before he had a chance to roll very far.

'Oh Jasper! I'm SO sorry. I didn't mean to drop you,' she said, stroking him tenderly. 'I'm so stupid. Are you hurt?'

'No, Star, I'm okay,' he replied, smiling mischievously, 'I bounce well, don't I?'

Relieved that he had not been injured, Star gave Jasper a quick kiss and slipped him back into her pocket, and then – knowing that she had already been seen and that there was no point hiding any more – stood meekly in the silent tunnel, looking around to see where the voice had come from.

The sight that met her eyes was one she would never forget. The tunnel had been quite narrow, but here it opened out into a sort of room cut into the side of the rock and facing her, sitting at a magnificent translucent pink rose quartz table on a sparkling rock crystal chair, was the most beautiful figure Star had ever seen – a lady in a long flowing gown. Both the figure and gown were a delicate sky-blue colour with white lace patterns, which Star knew was blue lace agate, and to her immense relief, she was smiling.

'Please sit down,' she said kindly, indicating a second rock crystal chair in front of the table.

Feeling vulnerable and unnerved despite the warm welcome, Star walked to the chair and sat down, lifting Jasper out of her pocket so he could see over the table. He immediately gave the blue lace agate one of his memorable smiles.

Expecting the chair to be hard, Star found it was surprisingly comfortable, but despite the blue lace agate's welcome, she was apprehensive, and some of her earlier fears returned. This was the first crystal she'd met, apart from the Sand Makers. Now she'd know…

Jasper, in his concerned, protective way, thought that the best way to help Star was to be as engaging as possible, and gave the blue lace agate another of his brilliant smiles, which she returned with a courteous nod of her head.

'Now, before we get to the formalities, please tell me who you are?' the blue lace agate enquired, though not unkindly.

At the word "formalities" Star's heart missed a beat. She hadn't expected there to be formalities. All she wanted was to take Jasper to the beach and go home. Formalities? That didn't sound good, but the blue lace agate seemed friendly, so Star coughed lightly and said, 'Please Miss Blue Lace Agate – you are a blue lace agate, aren't you?' at which the figure inclined her head in courteous acknowledgement. 'I'm Star, and this is Jasper. Jasper Pebble. We're very pleased to meet you, because we need your help. We've just been trapped here by a fall of rocks and we need to find a way out, so we can go home.'

'Star and Jasper,' repeated the blue lace agate, taking up a quill with what looked like a tiny diamond at its tip – and immediately the cause of the scratching they'd heard became clear. It wasn't a mouse, but the sound of the diamond quill scratching onto the rose quartz table! As the blue lace agate began to scratch their names, the table winced.

She put down her quill, and looked at Star and Jasper.

'What a nice smile you have, Jasper!' she said, and then, introducing herself, 'I'm Agatha. I am one of the guardians of the Land of Gems.' She smiled at them for a while, and then, becoming more serious, asked, 'Now, what brings you here? What brings you to the Land of Gems?'

'I... I'm lost,' replied Star in as brave a voice as she could manage. 'I tried to rescue Pebble – I mean Jasper – and... and then the rocks blocked the tunnel and we couldn't get out... and now we're trapped. I just want to take Jasper to the beach to be with his friends and then get home before my mum finds out I've gone. Can you please tell me how to get out, so I can go home?' she finished timidly.

Agatha replied, shaking her head gravely, but not unkindly, 'I'm afraid that's not possible, Star. Now that you've come to our world, you and your little,' she looked at Jasper, 'er... little friend must stay here.'

Jasper gave a squeak of alarm and – looking up at Star and then at Agatha – asked in a small voice, 'What? Stay here? For how long?'

'Forever,' replied Agatha, with an air of grave finality. 'Those who choose to come to our world, must always stay.'

'**Stay?**' cried Star in alarm, 'but I CAN'T stay. I've got homework and... and I'll be missed, and I PROMISED to take Jasper to the beach to be with his friends. I can't stay here,' she finished lamely. 'I just can't.'

'But weren't you warned to stay away?' asked Agatha. 'Weren't you told you would not be able to leave if you came here? Didn't you see a Mine Truck, and didn't it tell you not to come here?'

'Well... yes it did,' replied Star in a small voice, 'but it was rude and unhelpful, and I HAD to rescue Jasper.'

'But, nevertheless, it warned you not to come in here?' said Agatha, gravely.

'Yes,' replied Star meekly, 'it did.'

'Then WHY did you come here, if you knew you would never be allowed to leave?' responded Agatha.

'I... I had to find Jasper,' she replied, holding him with both hands, unable to stop her tears. 'He was lost. He rolled into the mine by accident. I... I just couldn't leave him. I couldn't. He's my friend. I couldn't abandon him. I only came in to rescue him,' she sobbed.

Star, unnerved by this new turn of events, looked up miserably at Agatha, her eyes wet.

Agatha leaned back in her chair, regarded Star's tear-stained face and Jasper's attempt to cheer her up by holding her hand and making smiley faces, and seemed lost in thought. Finally, she leaned forward and said, rather less severely, 'Hmmmm. So your little friend rolled into our world by ACCIDENT? And then you came in to rescue him? Is that what happened?'

'Yes,' replied Star earnestly, holding Jasper up for her to see. 'That's EXACTLY what happened. Look – he's got no legs. He couldn't rescue himself. He can't walk.'

'Oh dear!' replied Agatha, looking at Jasper's lack of legs and giving the matter more thought. 'This is all very irregular. Visitors to our world are never allowed to leave but... I suppose that under the circumstances you might... are you SURE he's got no legs? He seems to have everything else.'

'Yes! I mean no, er... no, he hasn't got legs. Look.'

Star showed Agatha again that, despite Jasper's little arms and hands, ears, brilliant white teeth and lovely smile, he had no legs, and then placed him on the table, where he smiled up at Agatha with the sort of smile that – were it an Olympic sport – would win a gold medal every time.

'But why did your little friend come here in the first place, even by accident?' enquired Agatha. 'How did he roll into the mine? How could this have happened?'

Star, desperate to make Agatha understand that Jasper had rolled in by accident, and that she had only been trying to rescue him when the rocks fell down and trapped them, began to recount her story.

'Please, Agatha, it was the Sand Makers' fault. They chased me down a sand dune and I tripped and fell, and... and Jasper flew out of my pocket and rolled down the hill very fast, and... and... and he rolled inside the mine. He couldn't help it. He's got no legs,' she finished timidly.

'Yes, yes, you told me that. You say the Sand Makers chased you, eh? Hmmm. I shall have to make a note of that,' she said, taking up the quill, at which the table winced in anticipation.

'But how did you get past the Mine Picks, who were guarding the entrance? They are very fierce. You must have tricked them to get past... '

'Excuse me!' Star broke in, immediately mumbling, 'Sorry, I didn't mean to interrupt.'

'Go on,' said Agatha.

'Well – they're not fierce at all! They stopped me at first, and then they had an argument about bears and tigers, and they both got frightened and ran off and left me behind.'

'Did they indeed?' replied Agatha. The table winced as she reached for the quill.

'Yes,' replied Star, with rather more boldness than she felt, 'they couldn't scare the skin off a rice pudding!'

'Hmmmm. Do rice puddings, whatever they are,

scare easily?' asked Agatha. 'I must make a note of that.'

The table flinched.

Having finished recording the incident, to the table's great relief, Agatha looked up at Star and said, 'Please go on. Tell me what happened next.'

'Well, I went into the tunnel to look for Jasper, and I found him in a puddle, and I was just about to leave when the rocks fell down and blocked the entrance and... and we were trapped. Please – I just want to go home.'

Star lapsed into a tearful silence, and Agatha looked at Jasper.

'Now what about you, Jasper? What do you have to say about all this?'

Jasper cleared his throat – and would have stood up if he'd had any legs – and in a clear voice said, 'Everything Star says is true, except she hasn't mentioned her bravery. I am just a little common pebble,' at which, Star shook her head, 'and when I rolled into the mine after Star was chased by the Sand Makers, I thought I would be there forever. But – with so much bravery that it takes my breath away to think about it – Star came into the mine and rescued me. Then the rocks fell down... and we were trapped. It's not Star's fault that we are here. It's mine. Please let Star go home. Please. I'll willingly stay here if you will let her go home.'

Star gave Jasper a tender look and shook her head.

'I'm not leaving without you, Jasper,' she said. 'Never.'

'Well, Star and Jasper, now that you are here, I'm afraid you **can't** go home,' said Agatha, not unkindly but with an air of finality. 'We're very strict on that. However, in EXCEPTIONAL cases the Great Sapphire does have the power to... er...'

'But I MUST,' wailed Star. 'I must go home. I promised Jasper I'd take him to the beach, and... and I must be home soon or,' she started sobbing again, 'I'll be missed.'

'Who will miss you?' asked Agatha kindly, noticing Star's tears.

'My mum. She loves me very much. She'll be so unhappy, I'm all she's got since my dad was lost. She doesn't know I'm here and she'll be sick with worry. I must go home.'

'And do you love HER?' asked Agatha.

'I... of course, she's my mum. We argue but... of course I... I... love...' Star's voice became firmer. 'Yes, I love her. I love her very much and I miss her. Please let me go home.'

*

Sobs wracked Star's body as she remembered all the wonderful happy times she had shared with her mum when she was growing up, and she looked at Agatha with so much sorrow that even Agatha seemed on the point of shedding a tear.

Agatha leaned back in her chair again, regarding Star and Jasper kindly, then leaned forward as if she'd made up her mind.

'Well, Star. I think that's all I need to know. I think your case may be special – though I can't make that decision myself. I don't believe that you came here looking for gems to steal, and I admire your wish to rescue and protect Jasper. That is a noble thing. The Great Sapphire is the only one who can give you permission to leave our world, and under the circumstances,' at this point Agatha smiled kindly, 'I think you should both go to the Great Sapphire and ask for permission to leave.'

'But... but can't I just go home? Please? Can't I find my own way out?' Star asked anxiously.

'No, Star. This is the Land of Gems. You can't just come and go as you please. If we allowed that – goodness me! All the gems would have been stolen long ago. No, you must go to the Great Crystal Cavern and seek an audience with the Great Sapphire. If he will see you, and believes your story, he has the power to return you to your world. You can tell him I sent you. That might help.'

'So I have to ask the Sapphire if I can go home?' asked Star miserably.

'The GREAT Sapphire, Star. The GREAT Sapphire. You must go to the Great Sapphire and ask if you can leave the Land of Gems. It's the only way to go home,' replied Agatha.

'Only... way?' sobbed Star.

Agatha responded kindly, but firmly. 'Yes, Star, it's the only way.'

For a while Star sat, head bowed, the silence broken only by her quiet sobbing and the sound of her tears splashing onto Jasper's head. Jasper was doing his best to cheer her up by trying to catch them. Eventually, realising that she had no choice, she looked up miserably. 'But how will I find the Great Sapphire? How will I get there? Is it very far?'

Agatha smiled and replied, 'You'll find the Great Sapphire in the Great Crystal Cavern. It's a long way, but everyone knows where it is. The Great Crystal Ball will be taking place soon, so you'll meet lots of crystals going that way and they'll be able to help you.'

'But how will I get there?' asked Star. 'Must I walk all the way?'

'No!' replied Agatha. 'No, it's much too far to walk, but you can go by train.'

'**TRAIN?**' exclaimed Star incredulously. 'Train?'

'Yes, by train. We're not uncivilised, you know. We have trains. Our trains are especially good, because every day the rail is taken up, and then put down again the next day, often somewhere else, so you can always find a train going where you want to go. If not today, then always tomorrow.'

'TOMORROW?' shrieked Star. 'But I have to be home for SUPPER.' And then, seeing that Agatha was unmoved by her outburst, asked in a resigned voice, 'How do I find this train?'

'Just go down here,' she replied, indicating the tunnel. 'Follow it and you will come to a station. You can't miss it. Wait for a train going to the Great Crystal Cavern and ask for an audience with the Great Sapphire. Explain the problem you had with... er... your little friend, and perhaps you will be allowed to leave.'

At the word "supper" Jasper had reached into his little winkle bag and pulled out a piece of seaweed, but Star, thinking it would be rude to eat in front of Agatha, admonished him.

'Jasper,' she whispered. 'Don't eat in front of Agatha. It's rude.'

Jasper held the seaweed, on its way to his mouth, out to Agatha instead, who declined courteously, and then reluctantly put it back in his bag.

Agatha then became very grave.

'Star,' she said, 'please remember this. And Jasper, you remember it too, because it's very important. In our world, you will meet many crystals and minerals who are charming, trustworthy and friendly – but some of them are not – and you must be on your guard to avoid the untrustworthy ones at all costs. You MUST be on your guard. Remember this – and you will be safe. Ignore it, and you will be in great danger.'

Her voice became even graver.

'Now Star, I must tell you this. You are wearing blue and that's not allowed down here, because blue is the colour of the Great Sapphire. You will have to change your clothes before you meet him, because ONLY the Great Sapphire, the little sapphires, and by special dispensation, the other blue stones – the lapis lazuli, blue topaz, the azurites and the blue agates – are allowed to wear blue. No-one, ABSOLUTELY NO-ONE,' she stressed, 'is allowed to impersonate a sapphire by wearing blue. Impersonating a sapphire is a very serious offence.'

Star looked down at her blue jeans and blue smock.

'But I don't HAVE any other clothes,' she said in a puzzled voice. 'How can I change them?'

'That you must work out for yourself, Star,' replied Agatha, 'but I do know that – if you go to see the Great Sapphire dressed in blue – you will NEVER be allowed to leave, and most likely you will be arrested and imprisoned.'

Star thought about this for a while. She really liked her blue smock and blue jeans, and blue was her favourite colour. She just couldn't see how she could possibly change them for anything else, so she let her thoughts move on to the bigger problem at hand – how to find a way to go home. She found herself stroking Jasper comfortingly – he was still making smiley faces and holding her hand – and wondering what to do. She didn't seem to have much choice. She probably couldn't find her own way out anyway, but if she went to the Great Sapphire, he might let them go.

'What do we do, Jasper? What's our plan?' she asked, looking down affectionately at her little friend despite her misery.

'We go to see the Great Sapphire,' replied Jasper without hesitation. 'He'll let us go, if we tell him the truth. You did such a brave and good thing, coming here to rescue me. He'll let us go.'

'I hope you're right. But I guess we have no choice. Come on then, little Jasper. It looks like we have a journey to make before I can get you to your friends.' She looked at Agatha, and said, 'We'll take your advice. We'll go to see the Great Sapphire, and ask if we can go home.'

'Splendid!' she replied. 'That's settled then! Off

you go, and good luck to you both. But remember my warning. You will see some wonderful things, but there are also dark and frightening places here, which you must avoid **at all costs.** You must be **very, very careful of the dangerous dark places.**'

'I will,' said Star, wondering what those dangerous places might be.

'Splendid!' replied Agatha, with a warm smile. 'Splendid!'

Reluctantly, because she would like to have rested a while longer, Star stood up and thanked Agatha. Now that she had come to terms with the fact that the only way home would be to see the Great Sapphire, her determination had returned, and with it the knowledge that the sooner they started the sooner they would be able to ask for permission to leave. Agatha, having accepted their thanks courteously, wished them luck, and then, having given Jasper a big smile in response to one of his, sat back in her chair and closed her eyes. Star waited for a moment and then, holding Jasper securely in her pocket, continued along the tunnel in the direction of the station. She couldn't help marvelling again at the thousands of tiny fluorescing crystals which lit their way, and despite the awful news that she would have to ask the Great Sapphire for permission before she could go home, she started her long journey in a positive frame of mind. However far it was, and however difficult, she would get there! She would!

'Jasper,' she said, 'we're a team. We're going to pull this off. We're going to see the Great Sapphire, and we're going to go home.'

Jasper smiled contentedly.

She hadn't gone far when Agatha called out, 'Star?'

'Yes, Agatha?' she replied, looking around.

'Don't let Jasper touch anything. Especially the little crystals.'

'I won't,' she replied, looking down at Jasper. 'You wouldn't touch anything would you, Jasper?' she asked.

'Me?' replied Jasper, shaking his head unconvincingly.

'Well, make sure you don't,' replied Star. 'We're in enough trouble as it is, and we have to rely on the goodwill of the crystals if we're to find the Great Crystal Cavern and see the Great Sapphire, and who knows how long it will take us to get there or how much help we'll need on the way. My mum is sure to have missed me by now. I'll be grounded and have no supper and... and...'

All her bravado of the minute before evaporated, and she started to sob, looking more miserable than ever, but once again she felt Jasper's tiny hand grasp hers.

'We'll be okay,' he said, giving Star one of his brilliant smiles. 'We're a team!' at which – despite her misery – she couldn't help smiling.

At the mention of "supper" Jasper had taken the piece of seaweed from his winkle shell bag and had started to munch, looking up between mouthfuls.

'Lesh go then,' he said.

'JASPER! Don't speak with your mouth full,' she

said, more severely than she really meant.

'Shorry,' said Jasper, gulping down the remains of his seaweed.

Chapter Six

The Journey Begins

With no sight or sound of a train or station, the tunnel seemed to go on for ages and after a while, to break the monotony, Star began a conversation.

'Jasper, what did you think of Agatha?'

'She was nice, but I was terrified when she said you would have to stay here forever.'

'Me too. If she hadn't told us the Great Sapphire had the power to let us go, I don't know what I'd have done. From what the Mine Truck told me, I wasn't expecting the crystals to be friendly, but now we know they'll help us, and the Great Sapphire will let us go, I feel much better.'

'The main thing is, at least we know how to get home now,' replied Jasper. 'It may take longer, but I know the Great Sapphire will let us go. You were so brave, and they must realise that we're only here because you came in to rescue me. I've never met a sapphire, but all the other gems I've ever met have been very reasonable.'

'You've met gems before, Jasper?' Star asked incredulously.

'Yes, from time to time. I was once very friendly with a chrysophrase, when I was in the Pacific Ocean. He was great fun! Bright green – just like those things in your garden.'

'In my garden?' she asked, not understanding what Jasper was talking about. 'What things?'

'The bright green things – on the wooden thing,' he replied.

Star had to think about this. On the wooden thing? The only wooden thing was the shed, and there weren't any green things on that. What could he be talking about? Then she remembered! Chrysophrase is an apple green agate. Jasper must be referring to her apple tree!

'You mean the apple tree!' replied Star, with a smile. 'The wooden thing is a tree, and the green things are apples.'

'Oh,' replied Jasper. 'One fell on me once. I was going to eat it, but some buzzy things got there first.'

'They were wasps, Jasper.' Star remembered Agatha's warm rich voice, and remarked, 'Jasper, Agatha's voice reminded me of my favourite aunt.'

'You have a favourite aunt?' replied Jasper in a startled voice.

'Of course, don't you?' she replied.

'No, I didn't have a favourite. There were too many to have a favourite,' he replied in a puzzled voice.

'What do you mean – too many?' asked Star.

'There were hundreds of them. They tickled when they ran over me.'

'They were ANTS, Jasper.'

'Yes, that's what I said,' he replied.

'No. Ants are different from aunts. Ants are small, aunts are big.'

'Do they tickle?' asked Jasper.

'Sometimes,' replied Star, remembering how her aunt tickled her feet until she screamed.

Lost in thought, Star continued along the empty tunnel, the shimmering colours from the fluorescing crystals transforming it into a wonderland. Jasper closed his eyes, dropped to the bottom of her pocket and went to sleep. The only sounds to disturb the silence were Star's footsteps and Jasper's snoring. Searching for any sign of the train that would take them on the next leg of their journey, Star was disappointed that the tunnel seemed endless.

Although Star was worried about what might happen on their journey, the encounter with Agatha had reassured her, and now she was more confident about meeting other crystals along the way. The Mine Truck had been right – but not in the way she had expected. She couldn't leave the Land of Gems unless she could get permission from the Great Sapphire, but she still had no regrets in rescuing Jasper. She knew it had been the right thing to do, and now the very rightness of what she had done would, she felt, carry them through to success. She and Jasper were a team, and Jasper had already shown himself to be very capable and intelligent, so she couldn't really imagine things NOT working out.

*

Eventually, Jasper woke from his nap and stretched his little arms in the air, and to keep her spirits up, she began another conversation.

'Jasper,' she said, as they walked along, 'did you hear Agatha say, when she was talking about the train, that they take up the "rail" at the end of every day? Why didn't she say "rails?" Don't you think that's odd? And what's the point of taking up the rail at the end of the day, only to lay them down again the next day? It doesn't make sense.'

'Yes, I heard that,' replied Jasper, 'but I don't know enough about trains to know if it was strange or not. I'm not an expert on trains.'

'That doesn't surprise me!' she remarked as she walked on, still mulling over what Agatha had said. Then she remembered that in many things, Jasper was knowledgeable and smart.

'Jasper,' she asked, 'why are you so clever?'

He smiled, and then went on in a serious tone of voice, 'Well, we're all made of atoms and…'

'ATOMS!' exclaimed Star incredulously. 'Where did you learn about atoms?'

'At school,' replied Jasper. 'All pebbles have to go to school, but for me it was so long ago that I've forgotten most things. But atoms – I remember about them! You see, there are only so many atoms in the world, so they have to be used over and over again – you would say "recycled". I'm not REALLY clever –

I don't have any legs and that's not very clever – but I must be made of clever atoms. At least, that's what my teachers said.'

Star smiled affectionately at Jasper.

'Whether you've got legs or not, Jasper, you are the cleverest and most amazing little pebble in all the world!'

Jasper smiled, and the light reflected from his teeth made the tunnel even brighter!

*

The passage continued to twist and turn as it sloped gently downwards, now and again passing smaller tunnels branching off on either side, some of them dark and menacing. Sometimes, as she went by one of the darker tunnels, Star was aware of a roaring, rumbling noise, like a great far-off furnace, and sometimes she could hear the sound of distant explosions, which reverberated through the tunnel and made the ground vibrate. Whenever she came to one of these tunnels she walked by as quickly as she could, shivering as she remembered Agatha's warning. After hearing a particularly loud and frightening noise which seemed to go on for ages, she felt a trembling in her pocket and noticed that Jasper was looking at her with anxious eyes.

'What's wrong, Jasper?' she asked gently, putting her hand down to reassure him.

'I'm frightened,' he replied. 'These noises scare me. It reminds me of the time I lived near a volcano. I don't have any legs, so I couldn't run away and when the volcano erupted I nearly got covered in boiling lava. I was very scared.'

'That must have been terrifying for you, Jasper,' she said in a very concerned voice, and then began to think about volcanoes and the lava that pours out of them.

'Jasper, did you ever see any peridots in the lava?' she asked.

'What are peridots?' he asked. 'I've never heard of them.'

'Peridots are little pieces of bright green volcanic glass. You sometimes find then scattered through lava like little bright green peas,' she replied.

'Oh yes! I don't know what peas are, but I remember little pieces of green. I was too frightened to take much notice, though. I was too busy trying to get away from the hot lava, wishing I could run!'

'Don't worry, Jasper,' she said comfortingly. 'You'll never need to run again – not from anything – because I'm looking after you now. I'm going to keep you safe and then, when we get out of here, I'm going to take you back to your friends. I promise.'

As Jasper looked up, gratitude in his eyes, Star noticed that there were crumbs of seaweed around his mouth. She took out her handkerchief and gently wiped the crumbs away, and Jasper, with one of his brilliant smiles, climbed up the inside of her pocket and resumed his usual position, peering out like a baby kangaroo. Before long, however, she saw that he had snuggled down to the bottom again and gone to sleep. Lost in thought, she walked on down the long, winding tunnel, silent except for Jasper's snoring, his little ears waggling with every snore.

Above Jasper's snoring Star suddenly became aware of another sound – and stopped in surprise. She listened, unable to make it out. She wasn't sure but... yes! There it was again! It was the sound of counting, coming very faintly from around a bend. Whoever it was seemed to be counting something, then losing count. Whenever it lost count it said, 'Oh bother,' and then started again. She listened, and heard, 'Twenty-one, twenty-two, twenty-three, twenty-four, twenty... er... er... **oh bother!**' and then, 'One, two, three, four, five... er... **oh bother!**'

Amused, despite her concern that she was about to encounter the unknown, Star continued to listen, and the more she listened, the more amusing it became.

Whoever was doing the counting didn't seem to be very good at it. They kept losing their place, and then starting over from the beginning, pausing only to say, **'Oh bother!'**

She couldn't help smiling. Intrigued to find out what it was all about, she nudged Jasper gently and whispered, 'Jasper. Wake up. There's someone up ahead, and they're counting something, but they keep forgetting and starting again. Let's go on and see what it is, but be on guard just in case.'

Jasper woke up, yawned and put his hand to his ear.

'Whatever it is, it doesn't sound like a train.'

'It's definitely not a train – unless it's got hundreds of carriages, and they're all being counted.'

They walked on, Jasper now wide awake and peering out of Star's pocket, ready for whatever lay ahead.

Nothing could have prepared Star for what she saw next! As she rounded the bend she saw another small cave cut into the rock, and beside it, leaning on a stick which looked like fossilised wood, was a very strange, ancient figure that looked – from a distance – like some kind of fossil. Star stopped abruptly.

'What do you think, Jasper? Does it look okay to you?'

Jasper stared for a while, then gave a reassuring answer.

'It looks fine to me, Star. I think it's a fossil, and it looks friendly.' Jasper smiled at her, and remarked, 'All the fossils I've ever met have been very kind.'

She walked on, and as she drew near, she stopped again and gasped – this time with pleasure. It wasn't the figure that surprised her – she could see now that it was an ammonite – but the sight behind was breathtaking! Star took a closer look, and was mesmerised by what she saw.

Inside the cave at the side of the tunnel was a pool, and cascading into this pool was a waterfall, tumbling out of a cleft in the rock above, but this was no ordinary pool – and it was no ordinary waterfall!

They both shimmered, glittered and sparkled with thousands upon thousands of tiny, smooth, sparkling gemstones, all of them giggling and gurgling and laughing with glee as they tumbled out of the waterfall and into the pool, in a dazzling rainbow of colours, turning the cave into a magical fairyland.

It was the most enchanting sight Star had ever seen, or could ever have imagined. The thousands of tiny gemstones, reflecting all the colours of the rainbow, were having the most tremendous fun. It took her breath away!

Enthralled, she saw that as soon as the little gems had cascaded into the water, they would climb out, march up some miniature steps cut into the rock, and moments later come whooshing out in the waterfall again, to tumble back into the pool.

The ammonite was doing his best to count them – or rather, how many times the little gemstones went down the waterfall – but they were having so much fun they didn't want to stop, and were doing their best to make him lose count. In a very good-humoured way, he kept calling out to them, 'Slow down! Slow down! **Rascals!**' but the little gems, clapping their hands and laughing even more loudly, did their best to make him forget even more!

He was so intent on his counting that he hadn't seen Star approach, and not wishing to interrupt him, she waited until he lost count again. When he came to the next "**Oh bother**," she coughed lightly to attract his attention, and then, introducing herself, said, 'I'm Star. And you're an ammonite, aren't you?'

'Hello!' replied the fossil, with a smile. 'Well, I WAS an ammonite a long time ago, but now I'm just an old fossil. I'm made of stone now, but once I swam in the sea and roamed the oceans, and I had a wonderful life. Now, my job is to count these little gems as they go around,' he replied, 'but I'm not very good at it.'

'I think you're doing a wonderful job,' replied Star, 'but it must be very difficult. They all seem to be having so much fun.'

'It IS a difficult job,' replied the ammonite. 'They are only supposed to tumble into the pool until they're polished, which is about two hundred times, but they are enjoying themselves so much I haven't the heart to stop them, and besides, I keep losing count anyway. This one,' he said, catching a tiny amethyst, which sat in his hand looking up at Star, emitting a gentle purple glow, 'has been around...' and then, looking at the amethyst, asked, 'How many times?'

'At least a thousand,' boasted the amethyst proudly.

'There you are,' said the ammonite. 'You see what I mean? It's not an easy job.'

Star, remembering that she hadn't introduced Jasper, pulled him out of her pocket and said, 'Mr. Ammonite, this is my friend Jasper Pebble.'

Immediately, the ammonite's face creased into a wide smile, which Jasper returned with one of his specials.

'Ah! A SEA PEBBLE! Hello my little friend,' he said, shaking Jasper's tiny hand. 'How nice to see you! We may have met before. From which ocean do you hail?'

Jasper, who had screwed up his eyes as soon as he saw the fossil, trying to remember something, suddenly replied, 'I remember ammonites!' and looking up at Star, said, 'I do! But now they are ex... ex...'

'Extinct,' finished the ammonite. 'Yes, sadly we are extinct and now we exist only as fossils. But tell me, my little friend, in which sea did you live?'

Jasper thought for a while and then replied, 'My last home was the English Channel, but before that I lived in most seas at one time or another. I used to sleep a lot and get washed from one ocean to the next, but when I got to the beach where I live now, I made so many friends I stayed there... until...' he said quietly, 'the sea and my friends all disappeared while I was asleep.'

'And that's why we're here now!' finished Star, giving the ammonite a brief summary of all that had happened to them.

When she'd finished, the ammonite and Jasper compared notes to see if they had any friends in common, but found they hadn't. The nearest they had come to meeting was when the ammonite lived in the Pacific Ocean and Jasper happened to be in the Indian Ocean – but this gave Star time to look more closely at the pool of sparkling gemstones as they frolicked and played, tumbling out of the waterfall and climbing up the steps to cascade down again with shouts of glee.

It was the most enchanting sight she had ever seen. The tiny gemstones were a kaleidoscope of colours and, apart from the purple amethyst, she noticed red garnets, pale green aquamarines, various coloured agates, yellow citrines, little golden topazes and a rainbow of others, all polished to such a high degree that they shone like little burnished prisms.

She turned to the ammonite and enthralled by the little gemstones, said, 'They are the most beautifully polished stones I have ever seen.'

'Yes, and the naughtiest!' replied the ammonite

with a kindly laugh.

'I used to polish stones,' Star went on, remembering a present she once had from her uncle, 'but nothing as good as this. I used a small polisher with a barrel – we called it a tumbler, because the stones used to tumble over and over until they were polished. I loved it. I even made some jewellery from the stones I polished.'

'Yes,' replied the ammonite, 'that's exactly what these stones are doing, except these little stones,' he raised his voice so they could all hear, '**ARE VERY NAUGHTY!**'

The little gems clapped their hands and chortled with glee.

Star reached out and caught one – a tiny yellow citrine. It sat in her hand, emitting a gentle golden glow, gazing up at her trustingly.

'You're a citrine, aren't you?' asked Star. 'What are you doing, apart from having fun?'

'Like Mr. Ammonite says, we're polishing ourselves,' said the little citrine. 'By going round and round and tumbling over and over, we become smooth and then we sparkle!'

'But you already sparkle,' said Star, wonderingly.

'Yes, but that's because the ammonite keeps forgetting how many times we've been around! We're only supposed to go around two hundred times. He's supposed to count us. But we're having so much fun that we... er... help him to forget.'

'**I HEARD THAT**,' said the ammonite. But then, as he was in the middle of counting, said, '**Oh**

bother!' and started again.

Star gently placed the little citrine back in the pool, and as she did, Jasper made a grab for it. He missed – his tiny arms didn't quite have the reach – and then looked up at Star.

'Can I have one? Just a little one?'

'No, Jasper,' replied Star gently, but firmly. 'I'd love you to have one, but they're not mine to give, and Agatha said I was to make sure you didn't touch anything. When we get out of here, maybe I'll be able to find you something nice.'

Jasper smiled a brilliant smile, and all the gems went, 'Oooooooooooh!'

The ammonite had counted to fifty when Star noticed that several of the tiny gems had climbed out of the pool, and were creeping away down the tunnel. They hadn't gone far when, noticing, he waved his stick in the air and called out, **'Hey, come back!'** at which the little gems scampered back and gleefully clambered into the pool.

'Oh bother!' he said, as he lost count again.

Star smiled. It was a gentle, happy scene and the ammonite was losing count with such good grace that she had a warm feeling that she hadn't felt since she'd decided to take Jasper back to be with his friends. She made a mental note that if she met any more ammonites, she would instinctively trust them.

The sounds coming from the shimmering pool and waterfall – and the tiny gems laughing and gurgling with glee – made Star want to linger, but she knew that she had to find the station, get the train, see the Great Sapphire and ask to go home as soon as she could. Tearing herself away from the magical sights and sounds, she turned to the ammonite to bid him goodbye, but he'd just counted to twenty – and the last thing Star wanted was to disturb him – so gave mental thanks for his kindness, bade him a fond farewell and turned away to carry on with her journey.

The ammonite, however, noticed she was leaving and called out courteously, 'Goodbye Star! Goodbye little Sea Pebble! I hope we meet again!'

Then – with another, '**Oh bother!**' as he lost count, he started over from "one."

Star smiled and Jasper waved his little arm as they carried on down the tunnel, narrow again since the polishing pool had been left behind. Star's heart was full of joy despite their desperate situation, and Jasper felt the same. In fact, he was humming a tune (not one Star recognised – it sounded like waves crashing on a shingle beach) and, from time to time, he looked up and smiled happily.

'We're a team!' he said, after he'd finished his tune, though Star wasn't sure that it actually HAD finished because it didn't seem to have a beginning or an end.

'Yes Jasper, we're a team!' she responded happily. 'We're unbeatable. What are we, Jasper?'

'Unbeatable, Star! Now, let's find the train and go home.'

With a light step, happy to know that they were on their way again, Star walked along the tunnel to wherever the train might be.

For a while, echoing down the tunnel, she could hear the ammonite saying, '**Oh bother!**' as he lost count, and once she heard, '**Hey, come back! Rascals!**' but the sounds soon faded into silence.

*

Star walked on, lost in thought, hoping she would soon find some sign of the train that would take them to the Great Crystal Cavern. Jasper had snuggled down in her pocket, and gone to sleep.

After a while, she grew uneasy. The tunnel was too quiet. Apart from the side passages with their distant rumblings and explosions, and warm smell of sulphur, it seemed far too quiet to be near a station.

Desperate to escape from the Land of Gems, take the pebble to the beach and get home to her mum, Star quickened her pace, but however fast she walked, the tunnel seemed to go on and on. Surely, she thought, trains make a lot of noise, and if there WAS a station, she would have heard a train by now? Agatha had told her that if she went down the tunnel, she'd reach the station. She knew that Agatha wouldn't have lied, but she still found it hard to believe that such things as trains – trains! – could exist down here, in this deep subterranean world.

More than anything, she just wanted to get to the Great Crystal Cavern and ask the Great Sapphire to let them go, and if she had to go by train, she hoped it would be soon.

Looking down tenderly, she saw that Jasper was snoring gently, his tiny ears waggling with every snore. She felt a great responsibility for her little friend, and was determined – more determined than she had ever been about anything – to take him to the beach and reunite him with his friends.

Her thoughts were interrupted by a sound, coming faintly but distinctly from further down the tunnel. One which made her heart beat faster!

As she approached, the sound was unmistakeable! Someone was shouting, **'Tickets please! Tickets please!'** and this was echoing along the empty tunnel.

At last! She thought. If there's a ticket collector, there must be a station, and if there's a station, there must be a train – and her long walk would soon be over. Agatha had told them the train would take them all the way to the Great Crystal Cavern, and that meant they would be home in no time! She began to walk faster, and nudged Jasper awake.

'Jasper! Jasper, wake up! I can hear a ticket collector! If there's a ticket collector, there must be a train! And that means we can get to the Great Crystal Cavern and I can be home for supper!'

Jasper yawned, and at the mention of "supper" reached for a piece of seaweed.

She hurried on, eager to find the train, sure that their quest would soon be over.

The Ticket Collector, when they caught up with him in the deserted tunnel, turned out to be a very impressive plum-red garnet, looking important in an official-looking peaked cap and holding a ticket collector's punch. Star was about to introduce herself and ask where the trains were when, before she had a chance to speak, the Ticket Collector demanded, in a very loud and official voice, **'TICKETS PLEASE.'**

'I... I don't have a ticket,' replied Star, rather taken aback by this turn of events.

The Ticket Collector, full of his own importance, seemed surprised and replied in a loud and incredulous voice, '**No ticket? NO TICKET?** Then you'll have to go back.'

He said this with an air of finality, pointing to the way Star and Jasper had just come, then turned his back on them and began to walk away, calling into the empty tunnel, '**Tickets please. Tickets please.**'

Put out by this rude behaviour, Star tapped him on the arm to gain his attention.

'Please sir, I... I can't go back,' she said. 'I have to go to the Great Crystal Cavern to see the Great Sapphire, and then take Jasper – my pebble – back to the sea. I was told to go by train. I can't walk, it's too far.'

'**If you haven't got a ticket**,' replied the Ticket Collector slowly and deliberately, '**you have to go back. Them's the rules**,' adding with an air of importance, '**no ticket, no train. If you can't show me a ticket, you have to go back.**'

After delivering this bombshell, he turned away and – still addressing the empty tunnel – carried on calling, '**Tickets please. Tickets please.**'

Completely unnerved by this new turn of events and not sure what to do, Star put her hand down to Jasper for comfort and then, looking down at her little friend, asked, 'What are we going to do, Jasper? We haven't got a ticket, we don't know where to get one, and we can't go back. What can we do?'

Jasper, who'd been regarding the Ticket Collector with the ghost of a smile, replied, 'I have an idea! Get his attention, Star, and let me speak to him.'

She called out to the Ticket Collector, and once she had his attention, said, 'Mr. Ticket Collector, Jasper would like a word.'

Jasper went on, 'Mr. Ticket Collector, if we show you a ticket, can we get on the train?'

'Of course,' said the Ticket Collector, as if speaking to a very stupid child. 'Show me a ticket, and you can get on the train.'

'What does a ticket look like, Mr. Ticket Collector?' Jasper asked innocently.

Immediately, the Ticket Collector lost much of his importance and became flustered.

'Eh? Er... well... a ticket's a ticket, isn't it? There are ordinary tickets,' he went on, 'er... return tickets, and then there's the other sort... er... seasonable tickets.'

Jasper looked up in surprise and asked, in an even more innocent voice, 'Don't you mean 'SEASONING' tickets?'

'YES! Yes of course, that's what I mean,' replied the Ticket Collector. 'Yes, that's what I mean – seasoning tickets.'

Jasper grinned broadly, and Star could see he was up to something.

'Yes,' he said, 'but what do tickets actually LOOK like?'

This was too much for the Ticket Collector, and he burst into a torrent of tears, collecting them in his ticket collector's hat until it overflowed and a pool of ruby red tears formed at his feet.

'I don't know,' he sobbed, and then – looking very miserable – wailed, 'I've never seen one. No-one comes down this tunnel. It's always empty. No-one has EVER shown me a ticket.'

'Ah!' said Jasper, in a sympathetic voice. 'I think I can help you there.'

He reached into his winkle shell bag, and after rummaging about pulled out an even smaller winkle shell – full of white sea salt – which he held out to the Ticket Collector.

'Here you are! **A seasoning ticket!**'

The Ticket Collector took the little salt pot and examined it.

'Oh **YES!**' he replied, looking more and more pleased. '**Very** nice. Oh yes! A seasoning ticket! Yes, that will do perfectly. Thank you!'

Having seen Jasper's seasoning ticket, his mood brightened and some of his old importance returned. He put on his cap, unfortunately still full of tears which cascaded down his face.

'Yes, that's a seasoning ticket alright,' he said, becoming much more friendly. 'It's all in order. Yes, that's valid for any train, and valid for you both.'

He saluted, touching his soggy cap and then – taking his ticket collector's punch and making a big show of it – punched a neat, star-shaped hole through the end of Jasper's salt pot. When he'd finished, he regarded his handiwork proudly, and then, beaming at Jasper, handed it back with the words, 'There you are! One seasoning ticket, duly punched!'

'Thank you,' replied Star and Jasper almost with one voice, though Star could see that Jasper was trying hard not to laugh.

The Ticket Collector nodded and was just about to wander off in his lonely search for tickets when Star remembered to ask, 'Please – where is the station? Where are the trains?'

He stopped and pointed down the empty tunnel. 'Not far. Just go down here. You can't miss it. Follow the tunnel and you'll come to a station, and there you'll find the train.'

Jasper, having enjoyed his little conversation with the Ticket Collector, called out in a very innocent voice, 'Um… what does a train look like?'

Luckily, the Ticket Collector didn't hear and Star was quick to admonish him.

'Shush, Jasper,' she whispered, 'let's quit while we're ahead. We don't want to upset him.'

Star was about to thank the Ticket Collector, but he'd already wandered off and was busy calling out to the empty, silent tunnel, '**Tickets please. Tickets please.**'

As soon as the Ticket Collector was out of earshot, she said, 'Jasper, that was BRILLIANT! Really, really clever! Jasper? Jasper?'

When she looked she saw that he had gone to sleep, holding his little salt pot in his hands, and was snoring gently.

Star saw that his salt was running away through the star-shaped hole punched by the Ticket Collector so, taking out her handkerchief, she wrapped it around him, stopping his salt from running away and making a little pillow for him at the same time.

Now reassured that she would soon find the train, she continued along the starry-lit tunnel, listening to the fading voice of the Ticket Collector in his lonely search for tickets, hoping the station would not be far away. The air seemed to be getting warmer, and as she passed one of the side tunnels she noticed a rumbling and a strong smell of sulphur. It was revolting, and she made a mental note to keep away from such tunnels in her journey to the Crystal Cavern.

By now, the sound of the Ticket Collector had faded and the tunnel was silent, with no sign of life – let alone a train. Star was beginning to think that she would never find the station when, without warning her ears were assailed by a loud and frightening noise...

Chapter Seven

The Mysterious Station

BOOM*! Boom, boom, boom!*

The sound reverberated through the tunnel like thunder, and then gradually faded away, leaving small echoes in its wake. Frightened by the sudden noise, Star stopped abruptly. Jasper woke up and asked, 'What was THAT?'

'I don't know, Jasper, but I think the tunnel is playing tricks on us. It could be a train. I read in my acoustics lessons that sounds can swell and fade inside a tunnel as the sound waves bounce off the sides, but that sounded really weird.'

'Whatever it was, it was loud,' replied Jasper, anxiously.

She walked on, more carefully now, worried about the noise and comforting Jasper, who was giving her some anxious looks.

'Don't worry,' she said, 'I'll keep you safe.'

Since meeting Agatha, the ammonite and the tiny

polished gemstones, Star had become much more relaxed about the crystals she might encounter on her journey. She felt that as long as she kept her wits about her she would be safe, but the booming which had just echoed through the tunnel like rolling thunder, didn't sound good and it worried her.

The noise died away, and Star came to a sharp bend. She hesitated, as she always did when she couldn't see what was ahead.

'Can you hear anything?' she asked.

Jasper listened, his little hands cupped behind his ears, and then nodded.

'I can hear a rumbling sound, but it's very faint. It must be a long way away. I can't hear anything else. I think it's safe to go on.'

Cautiously, still frightened by the loud booming that had shocked her and woken Jasper, she made her way slowly around the bend in the tunnel – and stopped in surprise!

Directly in front, was a much bigger tunnel, running at right angles from left to right, wider and brighter than anything she'd seen so far. It reminded her of the first time she went to London and walked into an underground tube station, except... except this didn't look at all like a station.

Although it was brightly lit and had smaller tunnels going off at each end, disappearing around bends just like the London Underground, there were no platforms – and no signs! Apart from a single bench leaning against one wall, it was just an empty tunnel, with nothing to indicate that it WAS a station except – and this made her gasp with surprise – right in the middle of the tunnel floor was ONE bright shiny rail!

Just ONE! Not two, like on every railway she'd ever seen before. Just ONE!

How could this be a station, she thought, with only one rail? Trains ran on TWO rails. If a train was perched on just one rail, surely it would fall off? She began to have second thoughts. Perhaps this wasn't the station after all. But what else could it be? She looked around to see if there was any way of finding out, like a timetable stuck on the wall, but there was nothing. The tunnel was deserted and silent and – with its single shiny rail in the middle of the floor – very mysterious.

Star looked to her left and saw the single rail disappear into a much smaller tunnel, which then went around a bend, and when she looked to the right, she saw the same thing – but however much she looked, she could still only see ONE shiny rail, right in the middle of the tunnel!

Tired from her long walk and confused by this new development, which was not at all what she expected, she went to the bench and flopped down. As she did, she heard a cross between a sigh and an 'ouch' – and immediately jumped up again. Realising that it must have come from the bench, she said, 'I'm sorry, I thought you were for sitting on.'

'Well I am,' replied the bench, 'but you... ah... I mean... you sat down rather suddenly. I wasn't quite expecting your... ah... weight. But please, do sit down. It's what I'm here for.'

Star sat down again, more gently this time, and heard a muffled, 'Thank you,' from the bench.

She looked around the empty station, and tried to make sense of it all. Apart from the tunnel from which they had just arrived, she noticed several other tunnels coming in at different places, all equally empty and equally silent.

'Jasper,' she said anxiously, 'this is really weird. It MUST be the station, but there's only one rail. If it's a station, HOW does the train stay on the rail, without falling off? Why doesn't it tip over?'

Jasper, who was very smart, but hadn't a lot of experience with trains, didn't have an answer except to say, 'It must be the station – what else could it be? Agatha said we'd come to a station at the end of the tunnel, and we've come to the end of the tunnel.'

Star had to agree, but was still at a loss to know how a train – any train – could balance on only one rail without falling over. It just didn't make sense, and she remarked, 'You're probably right, but this doesn't look like any station I've ever seen. Stations usually have platforms and people, and timetables and things and at least two rails. What do you think, Jasper? Shall we stay here and see what happens?'

Jasper's calm voice reassured her, and she saw he was pointing to where they'd entered.

'We came in over there, Star. We were told the station was at the end of the tunnel. This is the end of the tunnel – so it must be the station.' He peered over the edge of Star's pocket at the bench, and clearing his throat, asked, 'Excuse me. Is this the station?'

The bench, thought for a while and then replied, 'To know whether it is THE station, you would have to qualify your question with a name.'

Jasper gave Star a surprised look, and whispered, 'That's a bit philosophical for a bench, don't you think?'

Star was too bemused to answer, so Jasper looked down at the bench and continued, 'Thank you, that's a very precise answer. So – what is the name of this station?'

'It doesn't have one,' replied the bench, matter-of-factly. 'If you'd asked if this was "A" station, I would have been happy to say yes. But you asked if it was THE station – and that question has no answer.'

For once, Jasper was lost for words, and only managed to nod to the bench, but at least he'd found out – it WAS a station.

Star had to agree the logic of what the bench had said, but the philosophical aspects of whether an unnamed station could ever be "the" station didn't seem important compared to the fact that there was only one rail. She still couldn't imagine how a train could balance on just one rail without falling over.

Jasper had now recovered from his surprise, and re-opened the conversation with the bench.

'You seem to be something of a deep thinker,' he said politely.

The bench, who always took time to think before answering, replied, 'When you're a bench, there's very little else to do. A bench's life is a mixture of quiet reflection and being sat upon, so I have plenty of time to think.'

Jasper, who could be something of a philosopher himself, began to enjoy the repartee.

'Tell me,' he said, 'how do you know you're a bench?'

The bench thought for a while, longer than usual, and Star, listening to the conversation in a half-hearted way as she struggled to understand how a train could balance on just one rail, imagined that if the bench had feet, it would be shuffling them. Finally, it answered, 'One has to make certain assumptions. My aspiration is to be a table, but when I'm being sat upon, I have to assume I'm a bench.'

'That's very interesting,' replied Jasper – but before the conversation could go any further there came a loud *CLANG* from up the line and Star called out excitedly, 'Jasper! A train is coming! What do you think it will look like?'

She didn't have long to wait for an answer!

From inside the small tunnel to her left came another *CLANG* and a loud rumble, growing louder until it was as loud as thunder – the noise that had frightened her earlier. It was louder than the loudest underground train she'd ever heard, and she waited with bated breath, ready to put her hands over her ears. Then – to her complete amazement – a train came swaying around the bend on its single rail. What astonished her was that, as it rounded the curve and came into the station, it was leaning over, like a motorbike going around a bend, and when it hit the straight track through the station it straightened up but continued swaying from side to side, like a pendulum. With a *'whoosh'*, a roar and several more loud *CLANGS*, it sped through without stopping, and then – as it reached the bend at the end of the station – it leaned over so far that Star was certain that the tops of the carriages would hit the tunnel wall. They didn't, and the train sped on unscathed, leaving a big swirl of dust in its wake.

Not quite believing what she had just seen, Star watched the train disappear, swaying madly on its single rail, struggling to bring the threads of the experience into focus.

'Jasper!' she exclaimed, as the noise faded and the tunnel became silent again. 'That was AMAZING!'

And it was. The train was tall – much taller than Star – but very narrow, only about as wide as one chair, and consisted of six coaches, but no engine as far as Star could see. It just seemed to balance on the single rail, but when it went around a bend it tipped over, like a sailboat in a gale, almost touching the sides of the tunnel.

After the noise and confusion of the train rattling and swaying through the empty station, Star noticed that Jasper's little hand was grasping hers tightly, and when she looked down saw a frightened look on his face.

'Jasper,' she said, looking at the little pebble tenderly, 'don't be scared. It was only a train. This IS a station. You were right! But how it managed to stay balanced on one rail, I just don't know, and how it missed hitting the side of the tunnel when it leaned over is beyond me! Did you see the carriages?'

Jasper nodded, still looking anxious.

'Yes, I did. They were tall and narrow and full of thin flat grey things, and they were all making a funny noise.'

'The thin flat grey things were SLATES, Jasper! Slates, just like you see on roofs. And they weren't making a funny noise, silly – they were SINGING!'

It was true. The carriages, which each had about three compartments, were full of slates, all sitting bolt upright and all singing in wonderful harmony. As the train rattled through the station Star heard, even above the noise of the train, a wonderful chorus that reminded her of a Welsh choir. *How incredible!* she thought.

And then it came to her in a flash!

'Jasper!' she exclaimed, 'They must have been WELSH slates! Wales is famous for slates, and for singing!'

It all seemed to make sense.

'Jasper, that was AMAZING! Welsh slates! I wonder where they were going.'

'Yes, they WERE Welsh slates,' came a voice, which made Star jump up in surprise.

Startled because she hadn't seen anyone come into the station and thought it was still empty, she spun around.

Beside her, surrounded by a bright green aura and emitting a glow that gave the impression it had a green fire burning inside, was the most wonderful emerald Star had ever seen. An emerald – almost as big as her!

It took her breath away – and Jasper's too, for she saw his little tongue hanging out. She made a small curtsey, which caught Jasper off guard and shot him down to the bottom of her pocket, and for a while she stood and stared. Thinking she was being rude by not saying anything, she made another little curtsey, shooting Jasper to the bottom of her pocket again, and as she couldn't think of anything else to say, blurted out, in a voice full of wonder, 'You're an EMERALD!'

The emerald inclined his head courteously, and smiled in agreement. Star continued to stare at the shimmering, translucent gemstone, and Jasper, who had climbed back up to his usual position and was holding on grimly in case Star should curtsey again, gave the emerald one of his brilliant smiles. After a while, to break the silence, the emerald repeated, 'Yes, they were Welsh slates. Very fine slates too, the best we have, and also our best choir. They are going to sing at the Great Crystal Ball.'

Star, regaining her composure, replied, 'Mr. Emerald, I'm Star and this,' she said, pulling Jasper out of her pocket, 'is Jasper Pebble.'

The emerald nodded kindly, smiled, and went on, 'I'm very pleased to meet you. Jasper, you say? You look like a sea pebble! We don't see many sea pebbles down here – but what a lovely smile you have! Yes, as I was saying, they were Welsh slates and they are going to sing at the Great Crystal Cavern.'

'The Great Crystal Cavern?' exclaimed Star excitedly. 'That's where we're going!'

'How interesting,' replied the emerald and then, looking at Star's blue clothes, said, 'I don't think they'll let you in if you're wearing blue.'

'I know, but I HAVE to see the Great Sapphire,' she replied, 'I have to. Agatha, the blue lace agate, told me it's the only way we can go home, and I need to take Jasper to the beach and be home in time for supper or my mum will be frantic. I was told I could go by train. I was told the only way to go home is to ask the Great Sapphire,' she finished timidly, trying hard not to cry with the emotion of it all.

'That's true,' replied the emerald. And then, after seeming to be lost in thought for a moment, said, 'Well, I wish you luck. My train will come along soon, but that's not going to the Great Crystal Cavern, so you will have to wait for another, but you MUST remember,' he stressed, becoming very serious, 'don't, WHATEVER you do, take the NEXT train after mine – take the one AFTER that. That will take you all the way to the Crystal Cavern. I must warn you though, you can't go to the Crystal Cavern dressed in blue. You are sure to be arrested and I'm surprised they didn't tell you that before you came here. Blue is only for sapphires. We don't have many laws here, but that's one of them.'

Star remembered Agatha's warning about her blue clothes, but – what could she do? She didn't have any other clothes, and anyway, blue was her favourite colour.

By now, other emeralds were arriving and before long the station was a mass of sparkling, dazzling, shimmering, brilliant green. Most of them nodded or waved, and as they talked and moved, they cast bright green reflections on the tunnel walls which, with the tiny fluorescing crystals, turned the station into a wonderland of colour. Star was so mesmerised by the sight, she couldn't help repeating, 'Look Jasper! EMERALDS! I can't believe it! EMERALDS!'

'Please remember,' the emerald went on in a more serious tone, 'after my train has gone, you must NOT take the next train, but the one AFTER. This is MOST important. Under no circumstances must you take the NEXT train. That would be very dangerous.'

'After yours has left,' she repeated, 'I must not take the NEXT train, but the ONE AFTER. Thank you, I'll remember that.'

Star looked around the station, now completely full of shimmering emeralds, and asked, 'Do most trains go to the Great Crystal Cavern? There doesn't seem to be a timetable.'

'No, but there's no timetable because the rail is taken up at the end of each day, and then put down the next day – not always in the same place – so a timetable would be of no use,' he replied.

This didn't make sense, thought Star, and feeling a little exasperated, asked, 'Then how do you know where a train is going?'

'I was wondering that too,' said Jasper, who had been following the conversation with interest.

'Ah, that's an interesting question,' smiled the emerald. 'All I can say is that – well, we just know.'

Star thought this was not a very satisfactory answer, and responded, 'But how would **I** know which train to take, if there's no timetable?'

'Because I've just told you! You don't take the next train, but the one after. That will take you all the way to the Great Crystal Cavern. You'll be there in no time!'

Not wishing to press the emerald for an answer which didn't seem to exist, Star brought up the other thing that was puzzling her, and asked, 'Mr. Emerald, the trains have carriages, but I didn't see an engine. Where is the engine?'

'They don't have an engine,' replied the emerald, 'because they don't need one. The train knows where it's going, so it doesn't need an engine to take it there. It's obvious when you think about it.'

Star didn't think it was obvious at all, and said, 'But, surely…'

The emerald interrupted, 'When you know where YOU'RE going, do you need someone to take you there?'

'Well… no,' replied Star, 'but…'

'Well, there you are. What is the point of having an engine when the train already knows where it's going?'

'But…' replied Star.

Could it be true? Could a train really not need an engine if it already knew where it was going? She made a mental note to think the matter through when she had more time, but for the moment she thought the emerald had to be wrong, so gave up and decided to ask a different question. She was just about to ask how a train could balance on just one rail, when she heard a loud **CLANG** from up the line, and before she had time to think, another train came swaying around the bend and rattled into the station.

As soon as it arrived, going much more slowly this time than the one that sped through without stopping, there was a buzz of excitement among the emeralds. It slowed and stopped, and then continued to sway gently from side to side, and the station shimmered with green fire as the emeralds got on the train. The one who had befriended Star said, 'This is my train, so I'll say goodbye. I wish you luck – but please do remember that you MUST NOT get on the next train, but wait for the one AFTER the next train. That is really important! Whatever you do DON'T get on the next train. Good luck and... do try to find some other clothes. The Great Sapphire won't like it if you arrive in blue. Oh, dear me, no.'

With a smile, a courteous bow to Star, and a nod to Jasper, the emerald boarded the train, the carriage doors slammed shut and the train rattled out of the station. Star watched the last carriage lean over as the train disappeared around the bend and when it had gone, looked around.

The station was completely empty and silent.

Weary after her long walk, she sat on the bench and to keep her mind off her problems, turned her thoughts to the strange trains and how they managed to balance on one single rail. Somewhere, in the back of her mind, she thought she knew the answer, but couldn't for the life of her think what it was. There had to be an answer, because the trains did exist – she'd just seen one! And they did run on only one rail!

'Jasper,' she asked, 'how can a train balance on just one rail? Why doesn't it fall over? And why do all the trains go from left to right? Jasper?'

She looked down, and saw that Jasper had gone to sleep, hanging down with just one little hand grasping the top of her pocket. Carefully, she uncurled his fingers and eased him to the bottom, where he lay, gently snoring.

Star went back to thinking about the strange train, and was just pondering why it had to lean over so much when it went around a bend – when the answer came in a flash!

OF COURSE! Gyroscopes! The trains must use gyroscopes! That would keep them from falling over when they were in a station, and the rest of the time – well, it would be like riding a bicycle! It would stay up automatically when the wheels went around, because the wheels would act like gyroscopes! That was why – just like a bicycle – it had to lean over when it went around a bend. It must be a MONORAIL! Yes! She'd read about them!

The thought that she had solved the riddle of the train pleased her no end, and she would like to have shared it with Jasper, but seeing him gently snoring at the bottom of her pocket, she decided not to disturb him.

But something else did!

*

With a very loud **CLANG** a train appeared from around the bend and roared through the station, hurtling along, swaying from side to side as it sped through without stopping. She felt Jasper wake with a start and climb up to peek out of her pocket. As she watched the train disappear, Star caught her breath as it reached the bend at the end of the station, expecting it to come off the rail or smash into the tunnel wall, but although it swayed alarmingly, it roared on and disappeared from sight. As the noise died down she felt Jasper tugging at her pocket.

'Whew, that was fast,' he said. 'I hope our train won't be that fast. The last train I was on went much more slowly.'

She stared at him in disbelief.

'You've been on a TRAIN before, Jasper? Where?'

'In your garden,' he replied innocently.

'IN MY GARDEN?' replied Star, incredulously. 'When? There's never been a train in my garden. The nearest train is miles away.'

'I'm not sure when,' replied Jasper, 'but I was in a little carriage not much bigger than me, and it went round and round. Then it came off the rails and I rolled away.'

Star was just about to tell Jasper that he must be mistaken, when filtering through her memory from when she was very young she remembered that her brother, Peter, had played with a railway set, and sometimes he and his friends would set it up in the garden, using pebbles and twigs as make-believe freight. That must have been when Jasper, quite by chance, was picked up by her brother, to be used as freight in his train set.

A wave of tenderness came over Star at the thought that her brother, who was now grown, had played with her little friend. She smiled at Jasper, who responded with one of his own.

'Jasper,' she said affectionately, 'where DID you get those teeth!'

Star, still smiling at Jasper, suddenly had a troubling thought. Was the train that had just sped through the station without stopping, the NEXT train?

Did that mean that the next train to stop would be her train – the one for the Crystal Cavern? Or did the emerald mean that she should get the next train AFTER the next train that STOPPED? It all seemed very confusing, but the station was empty, there were no timetables and no-one to ask. Except…

She looked down at the bench.

'Excuse me,' she said, not knowing how to address it. 'Was that the next train?'

The bench thought for a while, and then said, rather philosophically, 'No, that was the last train.'

'Yes,' replied Star, 'but it didn't stop. What I mean is, will the next train that arrives – and stops – be regarded as the next train, or does a train that comes in, but doesn't stop, still count?'

'None of the trains count, as far as I know,' replied the bench. 'They don't need to count as long as they know where they're going.'

'Yes… er… no. What I mean is, which is the next train?'

'Every train is the next train. If a train comes in, the train that comes after it is always the next train, until – when it leaves – it becomes the last train,' replied the bench, without a trace of irony.

'Yes, I see that,' replied Star patiently, 'but what I mean is, if a train doesn't stop, can that still be regarded as the next train?'

'Well,' replied the bench, in a rather learned and important voice – for a bench, 'you have to qualify the term NEXT with the words "train that stops" or "train that doesn't stop". It's simple really. Without qualifying the term NEXT you can have no idea. Does that answer your question?'

'Er... sort of. Yes, I think so,' replied Star. 'Thank you.'

Star thought about this and – to her horror – realised that the emerald HADN'T qualified NEXT with the words "that stops". He'd said "not the next train but the one after" and with a sinking feeling, she realised that she really had no idea if the next train that stopped was her train or not. What was she to do? With a feeling of dread, she remembered that under no circumstances was she to take the NEXT train.

Star was still ruminating about this, but had come to the conclusion that she should catch the train after the next train that stopped, when she heard another **CLANG** and the rumble and roar of an approaching train.

This time the train slowed and stopped in the empty station, and – once the echo from the noise of its arrival had faded – remained balanced on the single rail, swaying gently from side to side, like a pendulum coming to the end of its life. Now that Star knew what to listen for, she could just hear a very faint hum from the gyroscopes which kept it from falling over.

She had come to the conclusion that the emerald had definitely meant her to get the train AFTER the next train that stopped, so she decided that this wasn't her train, and remained sitting on the bench.

'This isn't our train, Jasper,' she said, 'but we must get ready for the next one that comes in.'

For a while, there was an eerie silence. There was something hypnotic about the way the carriages, after leaning over as they came around the curve into the station, continued to sway from side to side after the train stopped, each time a little less than before.

The train was empty, apart from one black figure in the first carriage, and the carriages looked dingy and dirty compared to the earlier trains, so she was glad this wasn't her train. For a while she sat on the bench in the deserted, silent station, wondering how long it would be before the carriages stopped swaying. Then the strange black figure got off and walked over to where she was sitting.

At once, something about it made her feel uneasy. She was sure she'd seen a picture of it in her book, but just couldn't remember what it was. As it approached it smiled, but it was a creepy, oily sort of smile. Star wasn't impressed, and neither was Jasper. Apart from its unpleasant smile, the figure was a sort of dusty pitch black colour and a bit crumbly at the edges. When it spoke, it fizzed and crackled, and little sparks shot off a few inches and then disappeared. Altogether, it wasn't an attractive proposition.

Star regarded it warily, though to be polite, she did return its smile. Then, looking down at Jasper she whispered, 'I'm glad this isn't our train, Jasper.'

'Oh, but it IS your train,' fizzed the figure. 'Do come aboard.'

'No thank you,' said Star, 'I'm going to the Great Crystal Cavern with my friend Jasper here, and I need the train after this one.'

'But this IS the train for the Great Crystal Cavern,' crackled the figure, smoothly.

'No, I was told not to get the next train, but the one after. So I have to get the one after this,' replied Star firmly.

'But this IS the one after,' it replied, in a silky tone despite the fizzing and crackling. 'This IS the one after the next train, and it's the train for the Great Crystal Cavern. Now do hurry up and come on board,' it continued in its silky but somehow menacing, voice.

'No,' responded Star, 'I know this isn't our train.'

'But it IS. I promise you, it is. This train will take you to the Great Crystal Cavern, and not only is this the NEXT train, this is also the LAST train.'

'What do you mean – the last train?' asked Star, anxiety creeping into her voice.

'After this one, the rail will be taken up and there may never be another train in this station again. Now do step aboard or you may be stranded here,' it fizzed. Walking to the train, it opened one of the carriage doors, and then, beckoning to her, crackled, 'Do you want to stay here forever?'

Star hesitated, and Jasper, his anxious eyes peering up at her, shook his head.

'I don't like it, Star,' he said. 'I think we should wait for the next train.'

'So do I, Jasper – but what if this IS our train? What if this IS the last train? He said we'd be here forever.'

Star had a very uneasy feeling about the black, crumbly figure – a feeling she just couldn't explain –

and all her instincts told her to wait for the next train, but there was no-one to ask. Except the bench!

'Excuse me,' she said, addressing the bench again, 'Is this the last train?'

'It could be,' replied the bench. 'It all depends if another train comes along afterwards. If it does, then this isn't…'

'Yes, yes – I know all that,' she interrupted, rolling her eyes. 'What I need to know is – could this REALLY be the last train?'

'It all depends…' began the bench, but Star cut it short with a quick "thanks" and looked at the crumby black figure, who was still holding the carriage door open.

'I was definitely told to wait for the train after the next train,' she said firmly.

'But this IS the train after the next train,' the figure fizzed impatiently. 'May I ask you a question?' it fizzed. 'Did you see a train go by just now?'

'Well, I did,' replied Star, 'but it didn't stop.'

'There you are,' crackled the figure triumphantly, emitting a few more sparks, 'THAT was the next train and THIS is the train after. Now do come along. It will take you all the way to the Crystal Cavern in no time. After this, there won't be another train and you'll be stranded here forever.'

Wary and undecided, Star was appalled at the thought that this might be the very last train. She didn't really believe it – but could she take the chance? She certainly didn't want to stay there forever. She HAD to get to the Great Crystal Cavern, otherwise she'd never get home. Although beginning to feel unsure, she stood her ground.

'Who are you?' she asked, 'and how do you know this train is going to the Great Crystal Cavern?'

The figure, fizzling and crackling with glee in an eerie, frightening way, responded, 'I know everything that goes on here, so I always know where the train is going. Now do come along, this is the LAST train, and if you don't get on you may have to wait forever and you'll NEVER get to the Great Crystal Cavern.'

Star remained seated, defiantly holding Jasper with both hands, and when she looked down, saw that he was still shaking his head. But if this really WAS the last train, and they didn't get on, they'd be marooned. She thought about going back to Agatha to ask her advice, but it was a long walk and she was in a hurry to see the Great Sapphire and go home.

'I don't like it, Jasper,' she said quietly, 'but I'm worried that if this IS the last train, we'll be stuck here and never get home.'

Jasper, looking worried, replied, 'I don't like it either, Star. I have a bad feeling about it.'

'Now do come along,' the black figure continued persuasively. 'This is the last train and if you miss this, the rail will be taken up and there may never be another train in this station ever again. This is the very last train. Come along, or you may never get to the Crystal Cavern.'

As it held the carriage door open and beckoned to her, Star tried furiously to think why she was feeling so uneasy. Still undecided, she said, 'But I was told NOT to get the next train, but the one after, so there

MUST be another train.'

'This IS the one after,' fizzed the figure, becoming louder and cracklier with every minute, 'How many times must I tell you? You SAW the one before, didn't you?'

'Well,' replied Star slowly, 'I did, but it didn't stop.'

'Did you ASK it to stop?' it asked triumphantly.

Before Star had a chance to reply, it went on.

'No, I thought not. You didn't ASK it to stop, so it didn't. I promise you, this train will take you all the way to the Great Crystal Cavern. This IS the train after next. It's also the LAST train.'

'But why is the train empty, and why is no-one else getting on here?' she asked, feeling herself beginning to be persuaded.

The figure fizzed and crackled even more loudly. 'These are philosophical questions that we cannot answer standing in an empty station,' it said, 'but come aboard the train and all will become clear. Come on my child, step up into the carriage.'

'I'm NOT a child,' she said abruptly, to which the soothing voice replied, 'Of course you're not. I can see you're not. Now – are you coming or will you stay here forever?'

Star didn't want to stay there forever. That was the one thing she had to avoid at all costs. She would never see her mum again, never walk on the beach, never swim again and never be able to take Jasper to his friends. She desperately wanted to get Jasper to the beach and get home as soon as she could.

She looked at Jasper, who was still shaking his head.

'Jasper,' she whispered, 'if we don't like it, we can get off at the next station. We can't afford to take the risk of it being the last train and having to stay here forever. We MUST get to the Crystal Cavern. If this IS the last train, we're sunk.'

With that, she reluctantly walked to the train and allowed herself to be guided up the steps and into the carriage.

The door slammed behind her, but as she sat down on the hard stone seat, covered in what looked like coal dust, her memory burst into life and the feeling of unease, which had been troubling her ever since she first saw the black crumbly figure, exploded into a terrible realisation. She gasped in despair, and shouted, '**PITCHBLENDE!**'

'Jasper!' she cried. '**That figure – it's made of PITCHBLENDE!**'

Yes, she'd seen it in her book. There could be no mistake. And pitchblende – she remembered with a shudder – was an ore of uranium. And uranium was radioactive – it was horrible!

'**JASPER!**' she shrieked. '**Pitchblende is an ore of URANIUM. It's nasty, dangerous stuff. We're getting off – QUICK!**'

She reached for the carriage door, but another had already slammed shut as the pitchblende got on, and with a jolt that threw her back in her seat, the train began to move!

She was too late!

Chapter Eight

The Ride of Doom

As the monorail lurched forward, throwing Star back in her seat, her first thought was to risk all and jump off. She reached for the door, but as the train gathered speed and hit the first bend, it keeled over so violently that Star was flung to the opposite side of the carriage. No sooner had she recovered from this than the train hit a bend going the other way, flinging her back to the other side. Although she could feel Jasper sliding around in her pocket as the train leaned over first one way and then the other, she needed both hands to keep herself from smashing into the side of the carriage, and all she could do was shriek, **'JASPER, HOLD TIGHT!'**

The train wasn't going very fast at first, but as it came to each curve, and tipped one way and then the other, Star became disorientated and began to feel sick. After a while, to her immense relief, the rail straightened out and although the speed increased, the violent swaying lessened and she was able to grasp Jasper and take stock.

The carriage, in which she was now imprisoned, was narrow and tall, just wide enough for her to sit down, but tall enough for her to stand up – and was filthy. The seats and floor – and even the sides – were covered in what looked like coal dust or soot. There weren't any windows, just big square holes where the windows should have been, so the noise thrown back from the narrow tunnel was deafening and a fierce wind came blasting into the carriage.

The carriage itself was made of a greenish stone with red marbling, just like the serpentine lighthouse her parents had bought her on a holiday to Cornwall. The seat was hard, and the sides rough and unforgiving, and Star knew she would have to be very careful to avoid being injured when the train tipped over at the bends, especially as there were no windows to stop her being thrown out.

The relentless noise coming in through the missing windows as the train sped along the narrow tunnel was ear-splitting, and the twinkling, fluorescing crystals flashed by so quickly they were just a frightening blur. Star tried to call out to Jasper, but her words were swept away by the wind, and she had to content herself with holding him tightly whenever she could, smiling reassuringly when she saw his anxious eyes peering up from the bottom of her pocket.

How COULD she have been so stupid, she thought. Agatha had warned her to stay away from the dark, dangerous places, and the emerald had warned her NOT to get the next train – yet that's exactly what she'd done. She'd allowed herself to be persuaded, against her instincts, to get on a train by a creepy figure that had made her feel uneasy from the very beginning, and now – she was certain – this wasn't going to end well. She had to keep Jasper safe, but she also had to keep herself safe, and as the train sped on, these thoughts gave her the strength to face whatever lay ahead. She'd made a mistake – a bad mistake – and now it was up to her to overcome it and recover the situation. They had to carry on with their journey to the Great Crystal Cavern to ask the Great Sapphire for permission to leave – and that's what she would do.

Her thoughts were interrupted as the train, picking up speed, hit more bends and began its wild swaying again, first one way and then the other, each time throwing Star across the carriage. It was like being inside the pendulum of a clock, except you never knew which way it was going to swing.

She had to let go of Jasper and grip the edges of the carriage to stop herself being slammed against the sides, or worse, hurled out through the missing windows. Terrified, she glanced down to see that Jasper was hanging on for dear life, his eyes wide with fright, being tossed from side to side, gripping Star's pocket so firmly that his little knuckles were white.

The monorail gathered speed, clanging, clashing and swaying over points and switches as it rushed along the narrow but still brightly lit tunnel. Then a loud and frightening **CLANG** echoed through the carriage and it lurched to the left, diving into a narrower and darker tunnel, tipping over like a sail boat in a gale, and then oscillating from side to side as it straightened up. Star, feeling as if she were inside a gigantic bell, thought her end had come.

The filthy train, with Star, Jasper and the pitchblende its only passengers, careered along, picking up more speed as the tunnel dipped sharply, the noise deafening and the fluorescing crystals streaking by in a confused blur.

They raced on and on for what seemed like ages, swaying from side to side around bends, a thunderous roar echoing through the open windows, and Star felt as if she were speeding through the narrow tunnels on a motorbike with no helmet. It was terrifying, and the further the train went, the more frightening it became.

Just when she thought it couldn't get any worse, there came another horrible ***CLANG*** and the train lurched sharply to the left again, diving down into a new and even narrower tunnel. The sudden movement lifted her completely off her seat, throwing her sideways and banging her head against the side of the carriage. It was all she could do to stop herself being sick. She didn't even have the strength to scream as it roared on relentlessly, plunging down and down into the depths of the earth. Its speed increased again, and the hideous, disorientating noise beat at her senses until she was sure she was going to pass out. Looking down at Jasper, she saw that he was tinged with green.

Still the monorail roared on, lurching into new and darker tunnels, swaying madly as it shot around curves and bends, nearly hitting the tunnel wall each time. Then, when she thought she could take no more, there came another horrendous ***CLANG*** and the train lurched into yet another tunnel, lifting Star off her seat again. It felt as if they were boring a hole down into the very depths of the earth. As the speed increased, Star gasped with fear, closing her eyes and trying to prepare her thoughts for the end that was sure to come, but suddenly – although they were still careering along at terrific speed – the train levelled out and the noise disappeared.

Opening her eyes, she saw they were no longer in a tunnel, but realised with horror that they were going over a wide ravine. At the same time she felt a blast of hot, sulphurous air burst into the tiny carriage. Choking and gasping for breath, she looked down and stared in disbelief, then closed her eyes, trying desperately not to be sick.

Far below was a huge boiling, bubbling red fire – just like the inside of a volcano – with smoke and sulphurous fumes rising from the flames.

As the train roared across the bubbling inferno and the hot sulphurous fumes swept through the carriage, Star wondered why her life should end like this. And poor Jasper. Why should her affectionate, innocent little companion have to end his days like this as well? It just wasn't fair!

Eyes closed, holding Jasper tightly with one hand and struggling to breathe, Star was on the point of giving up when, without warning, they flashed into another narrow tunnel and the heat and choking fumes were replaced by the roar of the train reverberating through the empty windows.

Although the sulphurous fumes still lingered, the air became cooler and fresher and with huge relief Star found she was able to breathe again. For a while the train roared on and she held Jasper tightly, even smiling at him from time to time when she saw his concerned little eyes, but then the train dived downwards into yet another tunnel, lifting her off the seat again. She screamed, and tried to stop Jasper flying out of her pocket, wondering if this really was the end.

CLANG! The carriage tipped over violently as the train dived into yet another narrow tunnel, throwing Star back into her seat and crashing her head against the side of the carriage, and she couldn't help shrieking, **'Jasper! Jasper! We're going down... down into the earth,'** though she knew he couldn't have heard.

Overwhelmed by the noise and the violent swaying, Star tried to cling to some kind of reality to keep from passing out, but as the train continued its headlong rush into the bowels of the earth, it was all she could do to stop herself being flung out of the carriage. Faster and faster – faster even than Star imagined a train could ever go – the noise pounding her eardrums and the few lights just a faint blurred streak, their nightmare journey continued. She was sure the end would come as the carriage, during one of its wild sways, hit the side of the tunnel and was smashed to pieces, but somehow that didn't happen and the train continued its roaring, swaying journey to who knows where.

Several times they sped over more crevices and ravines, with roaring fires far below, being assaulted by the sickening smell of boiling sulphur and the choking fumes.

As the noise rose to a howling crescendo, Star was finally overcome by the fumes and violent swaying, and lapsed into unconsciousness.

'**STAR!** Star! Wake up! Star! The train's stopped. Let's get off! Quick!'

As her senses returned, she realised that the train had stopped and Jasper, tugging urgently at her pocket, was doing his best to wake her up.

As she came to, she found herself slumped in the grimy carriage, still swaying gently from side to side like a cradle being rocked. In the poorly lit tunnel there was no sound of any kind, and after the deafening noise of the train, the silence almost hurt Star's ears.

'Star! Quick, let's get off!' came Jasper's urgent plea.

It didn't take her long to realise that this was their big chance to escape, so with one hand holding Jasper, she opened the carriage door and dropped onto the rough stone floor, collapsing in a heap.

It wasn't a moment too soon! As she hit the ground, the train gave a lurch and sped off down the tunnel. Dazed, and still trying to recover her breath, Star watched it disappear around a bend.

Her first thoughts were for Jasper, but as she saw the flash of little white teeth from one of his wonderful smiles, she knew he was alright. The air had a warm sulphurous smell, but it wasn't as bad as when they were crossing the ravines so she could breathe easily. She leaned against the wall, her heart pounding, and tried to recover from her terrifying ordeal.

After a while, she began to feel more positive. She was alive – and they had escaped!

'Jasper,' she said quietly, 'that was too awful for

words. How we survived I don't know. You must have been so frightened.' She looked down tenderly at her little friend, who had had by now lost his greenish tinge and was looking better. 'I was so worried about you, but each time I tried to hold you I was thrown against the side of the carriage. I really thought we were finished.'

Jasper, looking grave, said, 'I was frightened for us both, Star, but especially for you. I thought you would be thrown out of the window, but I knew you would keep me safe if you could.'

She smiled and thought, *Yes, I WILL keep you safe, little pebble. We're a team.*

As the full impact of their narrow escape sank in, Star became reflective and said, 'Jasper, how COULD I have been so stupid as to be taken in by a pitchblende? How could I? You warned me not to get on the train.'

'Don't beat yourself up, Star,' said Jasper comfortingly. 'The pitchblende was very persuasive, and anyone would have done the same. I wasn't happy, but – like you – I thought we could get off at the next station if it was the wrong train. You have a kind heart – you proved that when you came into the dark mine to rescue me – and you are very trusting. You're no match for a pitchblende, but the main thing is, we escaped!'

Star smiled at her little friend and replied, 'That's true, Jasper. But I should have been more careful. I didn't like the way it fizzed and crackled, and those little sparks that kept shooting out scared me. I should have remembered what it was, and how nasty pitchblende is. Before they discovered it was so dangerous, it was used to make green glass, but when they found it was radioactive, and realised how harmful it was, they stopped that and now it's only used to make uranium. Remind me never to have ANYTHING to do with a pitchblende again!'

'I WILL!' cried Jasper.

'Now, what do we need?' asked Star.

'A PLAN!' cried Jasper.

'Right,' responded Star, 'let's think of one!'

She took stock of their situation. Although she had no way of knowing how far they had come, or how deep into the earth the monorail had taken them, she knew it must have been a long way and their main priority would have to be to get back to the higher levels, where the air was better, they could meet friendly crystals and ask the way to the Crystal Cavern. The question was – how?

'Jasper,' she said after a while, 'we need to get out of here, as fast as we can. When we left the station I noticed that every time the train dived into a new tunnel it went to the left, so... so if we go back up this tunnel and keep turning right, we should eventually get back to the station. What do you think?'

'I noticed we were always turning left,' replied Jasper, 'and logically you are right. But how can we get past the ravines with the boiling fires? And what if we meet a train coming down the line when we are halfway across? We'd be knocked into the flames, and that would be the end.'

Star had to agree.

'We couldn't pass the fires, I know that, but I don't think we have any choice. We'll have to go back, because going forward will only take us to where the train was going, and that's one place we DON'T want to go, wherever it is.'

For a while, lost in thought, Star tried to work out the basis of a plan, stroking Jasper comfortingly and from time to time receiving one of his reassuring smiles. Eventually, she decided they had no choice but to try and walk back the way they had come. Standing up, she inspected the tunnel, with its single rail gleaming menacingly in the dim light.

'Jasper, this is what I think we should do. We'll walk back up the line, following the rail, and we'll keep turning right every time we come to a place where the line splits. When we come to the ravines, we'll have to decide what to do. What do you think?'

Jasper agreed. It was the only possible plan, even though they both knew the ravines, with the bubbling fires below, were going to be a very big problem.

Having agreed on their plan, Star brushed the worst of the coal dust from her clothes, and holding Jasper firmly in her pocket, began to make her way up the tunnel.

'Come on, Jasper, let's put our best foot forward!' she said, immediately regretting it as she remembered that Jasper didn't have any feet. Then, with more confidence than she felt, said, 'We'll soon be back!'

*

They hadn't gone far when – to her horror – Jasper tugged at her pocket and called out, 'Star! There's a train coming! You have to get out of the way!'

Star listened, and although she couldn't hear anything, she knew that Jasper – with his acute hearing – would be right. With rising panic, she realised there wouldn't be room for her AND the train in the narrow tunnel, and if she was still there when the train roared past, she would be crushed to death.

Frantically, she looked for somewhere to hide, gasping, 'Jasper, there won't be room for the train and me. I'll be crushed.'

Moments later, she heard a distant **CLANG**, and then the rumble of another train speeding down the line towards her, and she shrieked in panic.

Above the roar of the approaching train, she barely heard Jasper's calm voice. 'Lie down, Star! Lie down.' And then moments later, '**NO! Squeeze in here!**'

She saw that Jasper was pointing to a small alcove cut into the side of the tunnel at floor level which, in her panic, she hadn't seen.

Terrified, she half-squeezed, half-scrambled inside, the noise hammering at her eardrums until she thought they would burst – and less than a second later, the train roared past in a cloud of dust!

It was a very close shave.

Star's heart was beating so fast she thought it would explode, but as the train disappeared around the bend and the noise subsided, she began to regain her composure. Crouched uncomfortably in the tiny alcove, she took stock.

'Jasper,' she said quietly, 'you saved my life again. Without your quick thinking and amazing hearing, I would have been crushed. I wouldn't have heard the train in time, and I never would have seen this little shelter. Thank you so much.'

Jasper smiled, his white teeth shining brightly in the gloom, and replied, 'It's nothing. We're a team!'

As Star's panic subsided, she found that the alcove was only just big enough to accommodate her. At first sight it didn't seem to lead anywhere, and she couldn't make out what it was or why it was there. It was very odd that there should be a small square hole cut in the rock for no purpose, but it had saved her life and for that she was very grateful. But now – they had a real problem! They knew the tunnel was too dangerous to follow, and would have to come up with a new plan.

'Jasper,' she said, 'that's another plan down the drain. Let's think this through.'

Becoming cramped and uncomfortable, Star began to lean back in the alcove, to rest against the wall, and try to organise her thoughts for a new plan.

'We CAN'T walk back up the line,' she said, 'the tunnel is just too narrow. We've used up another of our nine lives, and we won't be so lucky next time. We can't stay here, that's for sure, and we can't go down the line either. I just don't know what to do – or maybe we CAN still go up the line? Suppose, if a train comes, I lie on the ground? What do you think? Would that work?'

She leaned back further, expecting to feel the reassuring firmness of the rock wall against her back...

'I don't think so, Star, but...'

Before Jasper could finish, Star found herself falling backwards down a long, steeply sloping coal chute.

*

As she fell, head first and lying on her back, she saw with horror that she was in a tiny square passage not much bigger than she was. As she began to slide, she let out a scream.

Her first instinct was to keep Jasper from falling out of her pocket, but it was already too late. As she'd tumbled backwards, Jasper had been flung out of her pocket and, with a squeak of alarm, was now rolling away down the chute.

'Jasper!' she screamed despairingly, as she heard him clattering and bouncing off the sides of the chute, the sound fading as he disappeared into the unknown.

In one way it was lucky that the sides were smooth and slippery, because Star was able to control her speed by pressing her arms against them, but it also meant that nothing could stop poor Jasper rolling faster and faster until he hit the bottom.

Star was sliding down behind him, going as fast as she dare, but the claustrophobic little tunnel – disappearing into the darkness – was frightening beyond belief, and she was desperately afraid of what she would find at the bottom. Her main thoughts were for her little friend.

'JASPER!' she called, as loudly as she could, her voice sounding strangled in the narrow space.

There was no reply, and Star knew that Jasper

must have rolled to the very bottom and would never be able to hear her. Frantically, she tried to make her mind work. She knew the only way to find him would be to follow him down the chute to the very bottom where, with luck, he would be waiting for her. But who knows? She had no choice but to continue sliding as fast as she could, and hope for the best.

As she neared the bottom, warm sulphurous fumes rose up to meet her, and the subdued roaring became louder and louder. Star was distraught, but knew that this was the only way she would ever be able to find and rescue Jasper.

Despite her fear, she continued to slide as fast as she dared, but then – suddenly, and to her horror – the chute steepened abruptly and she found herself going faster and faster. Her arms, pressed against the sides, began to burn and she had to let go, hoping desperately it wouldn't last long.

Luckily it didn't – and with a *whooosh!* – Star shot out of the bottom of the chute, tumbling over and over until she landed in a crumpled heap on top of a pile of coal.

Chapter Nine

The Evil Pitchblendes

Distraught at losing Jasper during her long slide down the coal chute, Star found herself dazed and frightened, lying on a heap of coal, which – luckily – had broken her fall. She lay there for a moment, overcome by the noise and the fumes that were now all around her, but as her senses returned she began searching frantically for him.

'JASPER!' she called desperately, '**JASPER, where are you?**'

It was a forlorn hope. Jasper would never be able to hear her above the intense roaring, and even if he did, she wouldn't hear his reply. Frantically, she searched the coal around her, but it all seemed to be shimmering and out of focus.

She tried asking the pieces of coal if they'd seen a pebble, but gave up because they were quaking so much she couldn't tell if they were nodding or shaking their heads, and soon realised that they were trembling with fright, and this was what made them seem out of focus.

Jasper HAD to be somewhere on the pile of coal. Where else could he be? He MUST be there.

The problem was, she knew that he'd look just like a lump of coal, black from head to toe – but then the thought that Jasper didn't have any toes made compassion for her little companion rise up and overwhelm her. Completely covered in coal dust and soot, deafened by the roaring furnaces and the hammering of machinery, Star felt completely lost and miserable.

As the shock began to wear off, she saw that she was in a huge subterranean inferno of a cavern, hundreds of feet long and many feet high, with a row of enormous furnaces belting out noise, fumes, sparks and smoke not far away. From time to time she saw one of them tip forward and pour molten metal – it looked like gold – into a huge trough. The noise was deafening. Apart from the roaring furnaces, the cavern resonated with the sound of hammering and the clang, grind and whirr of machinery. Figures were scurrying about, silhouetted in the sparks and flames flying out of the furnaces. It was a scene of utter bedlam, like something out of a book showing the horrors of the Industrial Revolution.

Instinctively, Star knew this was a bad place to be. As soon as she saw the scurrying figures and realised she was not alone, she did her best to make herself inconspicuous by burrowing into the coal, and then resumed her search for Jasper.

He must be covered in coal dust and look just like a lump of coal, she thought, so how could she find him amongst all the other pieces of coal? The answer came in a flash!

His teeth! Of course! If he smiled – and he would if he saw her – she'd see his teeth gleaming against the black coal. NOW she had a chance! All she had to do was look for a lump of coal that, instead of shivering with fright, was smiling and waving at her.

Star had just started a methodical search of the coal pile to see if she could spot Jasper's teeth, when some sixth sense made her look up. To her absolute horror, she saw the iron bucket of a massive coal scoop moving towards her on a gantry. Mesmerised, she watched as the huge bucket came closer and closer, until it was suspended high in the air above her.

Instinct told her what would happen next. The bucket would drop down on its chain, the clam shell doors would open and then a load of coal would be scooped up to be taken away and dropped into a furnace. Knowing what was about to happen, but still somehow mesmerised, Star only just managed to scramble clear as the huge iron bucket hit the coal at the very spot where, moments before, she'd burrowed down for safety. The gears growled, and as the clam shell doors began to close, she scrambled away – just in time – and ran, heart racing, to the side of the cavern. Watching in horror as the bucket rose up on its chain, on its way to feed the hungry furnaces, she wondered if poor Jasper was inside.

Having slithered down the coal, Star stood with her back to the cavern wall, close by the coal chute that had brought her to this nightmare cavern, panting and gasping with fear. The coal scoop bucket moved away on its gantry, stopping directly above a furnace, where she saw – as if in slow motion – the clam shell doors open and the coal tumble into the fire. Frantically, she looked for somewhere to hide, feeling vulnerable in the flickering red shadows cast by the furnaces.

The coal pile, being quite near the furnaces, was well lit by the reddish glow from the fires, but further away, the cavern was much darker, and her first instinct was to run to the darkest part and hide – but then she thought of Jasper. Poor Jasper! She knew she couldn't leave him and would have to find him and rescue him as soon as possible, but although desperately worried, she knew that unless he had already been taken away by the coal scoop, he would be smart enough to escape danger by using his hands. If she could save herself for the time being, she would be able to make a plan and then come back and rescue him. Yes, she thought, the best way to save Jasper would be to save herself first, work out a plan and then come back and get him.

First, she had to hide! If she was caught again, she would never be able to rescue him, so – squeezing herself against the wall and trying to stay within the surreal patterns cast by the flickering shadows – Star decided to run for the darkest part of the cavern. She took one last look around to make sure she hadn't been noticed.

Too late! With a horrible feeling of dread, she saw a dull crumbly-black figure standing by a monorail parked on the far side of the cavern – the pitchblende!

Even at that distance, Star could see it was the same pitchblende who had tricked her into getting onto the train, and worse – it was looking her way! The pitchblende knew she had escaped, and was now looking for her. She felt it was only a matter of time before she was spotted, and then, who knows what would happen. Whatever it was, it would be very unpleasant.

With an involuntary gasp, Star ducked down and ran desperately for cover, away from the furnaces, dodging in and out of the flickering red shadows, keeping as close to the wall as possible. The further she ran the darker it became until, completely out of breath, she threw herself down onto the rocky floor, and in the suffocating fumes that filled the cavern, desperately tried to get her breath back. Had she been seen? She didn't think so. Thinking that she would be safe for the time being, she looked around.

Dazed by the sudden turn of events and distraught at having lost Jasper, Star tried to think of a plan. Although the situation was desperate, an inner steely resolve had taken the place of the panic that had overwhelmed her as she slid down the coal chute, and this resolve was now directed at saving herself so she could go back and rescue Jasper.

In the flames pouring out of the furnaces, Star could see figures scurrying around, and although the constant roaring still assailed her ears, she felt reasonably safe where she was, for the time being at least. Although it wasn't completely dark, it was darker than the rest of the cavern.

She continued to look around and then, as if in answer to her prayers, saw through the gloom a derelict stone shed at the very furthest end of the cavern. Without hesitating, she stood up and ran to it, hoping it would be a good place to hide, rest, and come up with a plan to rescue Jasper, but as she approached, her heart sank.

It had a door. What if it was locked? She ran up and pushed – and to her delight the door swung open! Thankfully, she ran inside and slammed it behind her, leaning her back against it to let her eyes grow accustomed to the gloom inside.

Perfect, she thought. As her eyes adjusted she saw a table and chair, and with a huge sense of relief, ran over and sat down.

Whew! That was close, she thought, trying to calm her racing heart and get her breath back. She had just begun to think of the best way to rescue her clever little Jasper when her thoughts were interrupted in the most horrible way.

'**Welcome!**' came a smooth, silky voice, fizzing and crackling with menace, from the dark interior of the shed.

Star froze! She recognised that kind of voice, and with increasing dread turned to look at it, desperately trying to focus her eyes in the dim light. Then – to her absolute horror – she saw a dark crumbly-black figure seated at another table.

With a sinking heart, she realised that she was once again in the hands of a pitchblende. It wasn't the same one that had tricked her at the station, but it was just as horrible – fizzing and crackling and emitting little sparks which flew off a short way and then disappeared.

'Welcome!' it repeated, in the same smooth, menacing tone.

Star didn't wait! She stood up and made a frantic dash for the door.

Too late! Somehow – she couldn't understand how – the pitchblende got there first, barring her way, smiling and emitting a shower of sparks.

'Going so soon?' it fizzed menacingly. 'Surely not! We have so much to discuss. Do please sit down.'

Star, completely unable to understand how the pitchblende could have reached the door before her, began playing for time. Unable to think of anything better to do, she sat down and glared at it. She was furious with herself for falling into another trap. Having been tricked once by a pitchblende, she had no illusions – she was now in for a difficult time. She sat in silence, her mind racing.

Perhaps she could appeal to its better nature? No, that wouldn't work. Pitchblendes didn't have a better nature. Maybe she could play them at their own game, and trick them? Perhaps she could, she thought, but tricking people wasn't in HER nature, and wouldn't come easily. She thought about trying to physically overpower the pitchblende, but that didn't seem possible either. No – she'd just have to use her intelligence and ingenuity to get the better of it. She desperately wished that Jasper was still in her pocket, with his calm, sensible advice and winning smile, instead of being lost in the frightening cavern.

Glaring at the pitchblende as it chortled with the pleasure of having captured her, she began to lose her temper and the angrier she got, the more confident she felt. Who were these miserable pitchblendes, who went around tricking people? HOW DARE THEY!

Star had worked herself into a defiant state of mind and was just wondering how best to confront the pitchblende, escape and rescue Jasper, when the pitchblende spoke again.

'How nice of you to come and help us,' it fizzed and crackled. 'We always need fuel for our fires...'

FUEL? thought Star, her heart sinking and her defiant mood evaporating. Fuel? What was it talking about?

In what she hoped was a brave and confident voice, she asked, 'What do you mean – fuel?'

Before the pitchblende could respond, the door creaked open behind him, and then she heard the voice she dreaded.

'How very nice to see you again!' it fizzed.

There, looking as evil as ever, was the very same pitchblende that had tricked her into getting onto the wrong train. In the same smooth silky tone it had used before, it went on, 'You escaped once, but you won't escape again! This time – we have you!'

Star felt her anger rising, and giving the pitchblende a contemptuous look, shouted, **'You tricked me! You told me the train was going to the Great Crystal Cavern when you knew it wasn't. How dare you! You always knew it would bring me to this awful place.'**

'Well, that's true,' replied the pitchblende, fizzing and crackling with the pleasure of having caught her again, and smiling at the other pitchblende. 'You see, we need fuel for our fires and it's my job to find it. I must say you were easily persuaded! Anyway,' it fizzed in the same silky voice, 'now that you are here, you must make yourself useful.'

'What do you mean, useful?' asked Star anxiously.

'We're going to put you in a furnace. We constantly need fuel for our fires, and you will burn well, so the next coal bucket that comes along will scoop you up,' replied the pitchblende.

'No!' shrieked Star, remembering the roaring furnaces. 'No! It's not fair.'

'Fair doesn't come into it,' said the other pitchblende, who until then had been silent. 'We have so much gold to melt, the furnaces must work constantly and we're always short of fuel. Of course, we use coal when we can catch it, but it's very unreliable – always running away – so we have to burn whatever we can get. You'll burn quite well.'

Star almost fainted. So this really was the end. She'd never see her mum again, never finish her homework, never go swimming... and never see Jasper again. Finally unable to control herself, she burst into a flood of tears, at which the pitchblendes became even more menacing.

'If you keep crying, you will be punished. We can't have your tears putting out the fires.'

'But... but, I don't want to go in the fire,' she sobbed, 'I want to find my pebble and go home. I only came here to rescue my pebble.'

'What pebble?' asked the pitchblende and then, remembering, said, 'Oh yes, I remember you had a pebble in your pocket. Well, it might melt, but it won't burn, so we're not interested in your pebble.'

'But **I** am,' wailed Star. 'He's my friend. He's lost and I have to find him. That's what friends are for – don't you know that? Don't you have any sympathy?'

At this remark, the two pitchblendes made a show of pretending not to know what a friend was – or perhaps they really didn't know. One said, 'Frens? Frinds?' in a mock-puzzled voice. 'No, never heard of that, and as for sympathy…'

It turned to the other pitchblende, and enquired, 'You ever heard of sympathy?'

The pitchblende shook its head, 'No, haven't heard of that, either.'

Star, despite her anguish, gave them a contemptuous look, and went on, 'Anyway, I'm on my way to see the Great Sapphire and I'm sure HE will have sympathy for me.'

As soon as Star mentioned the Great Sapphire there was a sharp intake of breath, and the two pitchblendes exchanged worried glances.

'The Great Sapphire?' asked one pitchblende, pretending to be off-hand, but looking worried.

'Yes, the Great Sapphire,' replied Star. 'I am on my way to see the Great Sapphire. He lives in the Crystal Cavern.'

'Yes, yes,' said the other pitchblende, irritably, 'we know where he lives.'

'So don't put me in the flames,' she continued as bravely as she could, 'or he'll not be pleased.'

The two pitchblendes exchanged nervous looks.

'Do you have an APPOINTMENT with the Great

Sapphire? Are you expected?' asked the first pitchblende.

Star had to think quickly. *Do I tell a lie, and say I am? No.* She dismissed this suggestion. Even in this awful situation, she had to tell the truth, because that's the way she was,

'Well, not exactly,' she said, 'but Agatha, the blue lace agate, told me to go, and... and...'

'Does anyone else know you are going to see the Great Sapphire?' inquired the first pitchblende solicitously.

'Yes, an emerald!' replied Star. 'I met some emeralds at the station and... and... a garnet collecting tickets. So lots of crystals know I'm going,' she finished lamely.

The two pitchblendes whispered together for a while, and then turned to Star. Her spirits soared as she saw they were both smiling benevolently.

'Well, this is all very interesting! You are going to see the Great Sapphire!' said the first pitchblende, fizzing and crackling. 'That IS interesting!' Then it went on, with a smile and the same benevolent expression, 'But you're not expected! He doesn't KNOW you're coming! And no-one else knows! And no-one knows you're here!'

'Except us – AND WE WON'T TELL!' replied the other with a laugh, nodding towards its companion. 'So that makes it even MORE important that we throw you into the flames!' Clearly enjoying their little joke, it went on, 'You'll be in the next bucket, and then you'll be warm and cosy. For a little while, anyway. Then you'll be very hot!'

Star came down to earth with a bang. The pitchblendes were smiling and joking – because they were going to throw her into the flames! How nasty could they get? She wondered if these were the nastiest creatures ever invented, and came to the conclusion they were. The pitchblendes resumed their whispering, still smiling at each other, and occasionally at Star, until one inclined its head in a very theatrical way, and cupping its hand by its ear said, 'Is that a BUCKET I hear coming?'

To which the other replied, in the same theatrical way, 'I DO believe it IS!'

The pitchblendes emitted a profusion of sparks as they enjoyed their little joke, and then one turned to her, and with a small bow that in other circumstances would have been regarded as courteous, said, 'Mustn't keep the fires waiting.'

'Certainly not,' replied the other, 'that would never do.'

Before Star had time to think, her arms were pinned to her sides and she was marched out between the two pitchblendes. As she left the relative quiet of the shed and was taken towards the pile of coal, the cacophony of noise – the hammering of anvils and the roar of the furnaces – began to overwhelm her again. She watched with horror as the bucket moved slowly towards her on its gantry, ready to take her and the next scoop of coal to the furnaces.

The air was hot and sulphurous, with sparks and flames shooting out of the roaring fires in all directions, and as she was marched towards the coal, she was desperately trying to think of a way out of this awful situation, trying to come up with a plan that would get her away from the pitchblendes – but held fast between them and unable to escape, she could only watch as the bucket – as if in slow motion – stopped and then, with a clank, began to drop down to the coal. As it fell, the gears on the clam shell doors growled and the doors opened.

Just as the bucket was about to hit the coal, Star was thrown violently onto the pile by the pitchblendes, landing just under the open doors. Screaming, she tried to crawl away, but already the gears were growling and the clam shell doors beginning to close. In the very last second, knowing that if she were caught between the iron doors she would be crushed to death, Star clambered inside the bucket.

The last thing she saw, as the doors closed around her, was the sight of the pitchblendes, fizzing and crackling with pleasure, smiling as they waved her goodbye.

Chapter Ten

Jasper Saves the Day!

Having been trapped inside the coal scoop, Star could see from the light filtering through the crack in the doors where they didn't quite meet, that she was sitting on a pile of coal, right in the middle of the bucket. She tried to prise the heavy iron doors open, but it was hopeless – they wouldn't budge.

She had to face the fact that there was no escape, and in a few minutes she would be dropped into a furnace. She was trapped, and that was that. She was about to meet her end.

Seeing the pieces of coal trembling with fright even more than before, she wished there was some way she could save them from what was about to happen.

With a sinking heart, she felt the bucket lurch as it began to rise up on its chain and knew that it would just be a matter of moments before the gantry took it away, to stop above an open furnace. Then the gears would growl, the clam shell doors would open – and she would be dropped into oblivion. Horrified, she wondered what it would be like to be roasted alive, and hoped the end would be quick.

The bucket stopped rising and she felt it swing for a moment. Time began to pass more slowly, and she reflected upon her short life.

So this was it. This really was the end. She choked with grief to think that her mum would never know what had happened to her, and felt that the pain she was about to suffer was nothing compared to how her mum would suffer for the rest of her life at her loss. And dear Jasper – affectionate, clever, loyal Jasper, with the most wonderful smile in the world. She would never see him again.

With a feeling of complete despair, she felt the bucket swing slightly as it moved towards the furnaces. The roar of the flames became deafening, and she knew it would only be a matter of seconds before the bucket would stop, the gears would growl, the clam shell doors would open and she would drop forever into the flames.

The big scoop lurched again as it stopped above a furnace, and Star spent her last few moments thinking about Jasper, who had saved her life when the roof of the abandoned mine caved in, and who had been a true companion through all their adventures. He was gone, and now he'd never be rescued. His fate would be the same as hers – scooped up from the pile of coal and then, with a sickening finality, dropped into a furnace to disappear forever. With his compassion, his intelligence and his wonderful, innocent smile, he didn't deserve this. Above all, she was sorry that she hadn't been able to say goodbye.

She wished she'd been able to thank him for all he had done for her. Dear Jasper – just an ordinary sea pebble, but so clever and calm, and so cute and endearing with his wonderful smile and sparkling white teeth. His tiny ears and eyes heard and saw things long before she did, and this had saved her life on more than one occasion. She remembered how, because he didn't have any legs, he had to ride in her smock pocket, and smiled at the thought of him peering out like a baby kangaroo, interested in everything he saw. And when he fell asleep, she had loved the way his little ears waggled as he snored.

But now, all that was gone and her life was about to end. Jasper was lost, and probably wouldn't last long either. It was all so unfair – Star was only in this mess because she'd had the courage to rescue him when he rolled into the abandoned mine. It wasn't HER fault that the mine collapsed, trapping them both.

Okay, she'd been warned to stay away from the dangerous dark places, but she'd been tricked by an evil pitchblende, and now here she was, about to be dropped into a furnace by that very same pitchblende.

With a feeling of complete despair, nearly fainting from the intense heat, she listened to the roar of the flames and knew the end was near. Although petrified by the thought of what was about to happen, she was able to say a mental farewell to those who had loved her – her mum, dad, Jasper, her brother and her close friends. Then, eyes closed, and thankful for the happy memories she'd had in her short life, Star waited for the end.

It didn't come.

She heard the gears begin to growl – but then, with a *clunk*, they jammed – and the bucket didn't open. For a moment it hung there, swinging above the flames. The second time she heard the gears growl, Star was sure the doors would open – but they didn't. Instead, there came another *clunk* as the gears jammed, and again the bucket stayed shut.

She didn't understand what was happening. Why should the gears on the big iron bucket jam at this very moment? By rights she should now be history, burnt in the flames and gone forever. On the edge of consciousness from the fierce heat, she waited.

Again the gears growled, but once more there came a *clunk* and the doors remained shut.

By now, it was so hot inside the bucket that Star, in her half-dazed state, began to wish that the doors WOULD open and get it over with – a quick end would be better than being roasted alive inside an iron bucket. Again she heard the gears growl, but again there came a *clunk* as they jammed, and the bucket remained closed.

The sides of the coal scoop were now almost red hot and Star couldn't take much more. Slipping in and out of consciousness, she heard the gears growl again and hoped the doors would open – but they didn't.

Instead, she felt the bucket lurch and to her amazement, felt it begin to move. Gathering speed, it passed over one furnace after another until it reached the end of the gantry, where – cooling down rapidly – it jolted and stopped high above the ground, swinging to and fro on its chain. Almost unable to believe what had happened, Star began to hope that her life would be spared a little longer.

She realised that something had gone wrong with the gears that opened the clam shell doors, and guessed that they had become jammed – perhaps by a piece of the gear wheel which had broken off. Whatever it was, the chances of the gears jamming at that precise moment, to save her life, were impossible to calculate. It was only a temporary reprieve, but at least she was still alive – and if she were alive, she might just have a chance to escape! She was just thinking how wonderful this would be, when she felt the bucket begin to fall.

It dropped freely, plunging down until it smashed into the ground, sending the coal – and Star – flying in all directions. Shocked at having been churned around inside her iron prison, Star dimly heard the gears growl and gathered her wits in case the doors should open – but they didn't. Dazed and winded, she instinctively knew that the pitchblendes were trying to free the gears – and having failed once would try again.

She was right. The bucket rose higher and higher, until it reached the very top of the gantry, poised as high as it could go. She braced herself for what she knew was coming. It was just as well she did, because this time the bucket plunged down at huge speed, crashing onto the hard rock floor with tremendous force, churning her around as if she were in a giant, malevolent spin dryer.

This time it worked. As it smashed into the ground, Star heard something fall out of the gears and clatter down the outside of the bucket, and knew that – next time – the doors would open.

And they did! The gears growled, the clam shell doors opened and Star and the coal fell onto the floor in a black heap of confusion.

Disorientated by the noise and her narrow escape, and still winded from the bucket's fierce landing, Star lay amongst the pieces of coal, trying to focus her mind. She'd been through a horrible ordeal, and faced danger with a bravery far beyond her years, but it had taken its toll and for a time she was too dazed to know what to do. Suddenly, she heard the gears growl, bringing her back to her senses, and in a flash she realised that she had to get away before the doors closed around her again, trapping her inside. Desperately, she threw herself sideways, and just managed to scramble clear as the iron doors, missing her by a hair's breadth, slammed shut. With a pounding heart, she watched the coal bucket rise up to the gantry and move off for its next load.

Dazed and disoriented after her amazing escape, she watched as the pieces of coal began scurrying away, and as her senses came rushing back, she knew she had to do the same.

Black from head to foot with coal dust and frightened – but determined to find Jasper as soon as she could – she looked wildly around for somewhere to hide. The bucket had smashed into the ground in a dark part of the cavern, but in the distance she could see the wall, lit by the flickering red shadows from the flames spewing out of the furnaces, and decided this was her best bet. She'd run to the wall and hide in the shadows, and then – once she'd made a plan – would go back to the coal heap and find Jasper. Having made her decision, she stood up and was just about to start running when something made her stop dead in her tracks.

'Star! Star!'

Wondering if her mind was playing tricks, Star looked down at the coal, most of it now making its escape.

'Star! It's me!' came the voice again.

Star stared in the direction of the voice, still not seeing anything but the scurrying pieces of coal, unable to take it in and not daring to hope.

'Star! I'm here!'

This time, to her complete amazement and delight, she saw him!

Looking for all the world like a piece of coal – but with his little white teeth shining brightly in the gloom – was Jasper!

'Jasper!' she shrieked, running over and picking him up. 'Jasper!'

It was all she could say.

She hugged him tenderly, all thoughts of her desperate situation forgotten. She couldn't find words to express her joy, but eventually, through tears of happiness and relief, she asked, 'Jasper – where have you been? You were lost. What happened? How did you get here?'

'I'll tell you later,' came his calm, reassuring voice, 'but for now – let's get out of here. Quick! **Run!**'

Star needed no second bidding! Putting Jasper into her smock pocket and holding him so tightly that he squeaked, and doing her best to avoid the pieces of coal which, with their short legs, couldn't run very fast, Star ran for all she was worth. Out of breath, she finally stopped in a small niche in the rock wall, deep in the shadows. Looking back, she saw the roaring furnaces and a group of pitchblendes gathered around the coal scoop bucket, examining it.

Taking Jasper out of her pocket, she kissed his grimy cheek affectionately, and as soon as her breath came back, asked, 'HOW did you get here, Jasper? I thought you were lost on the coal pile.' Before he had a chance to answer, the reality of her narrow escape sank home, and she went on. 'WHAT an ordeal, Jasper! Something jammed the gears and stopped the doors opening. It was a MIRACLE! How DID I get out of **THAT?**'

In disbelief, she heard Jasper's modest reply, '**I jammed the mechanism.**'

'You did **WHAT?**' asked Star in amazement.

'I jammed the gears,' replied Jasper, rubbing his side. I saw you being thrown onto the coal by those horrible pitchblendes. I could see the bucket was going to scoop you up and take you away, so when the doors closed, I pushed myself into the gears so they wouldn't open again.'

Star gazed at Jasper in disbelief. This lovely, modest little pebble had, by his quick thinking and bravery, just saved her life – AGAIN!

'Jasper, I am lost for words,' she said. 'You are wonderful! You just saved my life, but...'

Noticing that he was rubbing his side and wincing, she cried, 'Jasper! You're hurt!'

'It's not much. It's only a chip, look,' he said bravely, showing Star a nasty chip in his otherwise smooth side. 'When I fell into the gears, I got crushed in the mechanism.'

He smiled, showing teeth which shone even more brilliantly from his coal black face.

'It's only a chip. I'm okay.'

For a long time Star hugged him tenderly, tears of happiness leaving white streaks down her grimy face. Eventually, she said, 'Jasper, you saved my life. Without you, I would have been burnt to a crisp. How can I ever, ever repay you, my dear little Jasper Pebble?'

Jasper looked pleased, but in his usual modest way, said, 'It was nothing. It's what friends are for. You would have done the same for me.'

A surge of tenderness came over Star. She kissed his cheek and tried to wipe the coal dust from his face, but even after she'd finished he still looked like a lump of coal with teeth.

'Right, Jasper,' she said with more determination than she had felt for a very long time, 'it's time to get out of here! We need to find our way back so we can go to the Great Crystal Cavern and ask the Great Sapphire to let us go home. So – what do we need?'

'A **PLAN!**' responded Jasper, happily.

To find out what happens next, and see what other heart-stopping adventures Star and Jasper have in the Land of Gems, read Book Two of the Trilogy – **The Raging Torrent**

To find out if Star and Jasper finally get to the Great Crystal Cavern, and how their adventure ends, read Book Three of the Trilogy – **The Crystal Cavern**

For an illustrated colour glossary of the gemstones and crystals mentioned in the trilogy, and other exciting information, visit Star and Jasper's website

StarJasper.com

12656205R00103

Printed in Poland
by Amazon Fulfillment
Poland Sp. z o.o., Wrocław